The Shacklebolt Messages

TODD MARTIN

To my loving wife Mary, thank you for your patience and for being a sounding board during the writing of this book.

Pinegrub, My Newest Tempter,

You may consider this your formal welcome into the ranks of the tempters. You have done well in your centuries of service as a minor messenger. The timely delivery of your last message to lieutenant Kormung and your servile attitude are the things that won you favor.

Kormung was able to finish the corruption of a human soul just before his charge's demise. He was well pleased and expressed that your attitude of urgency greatly aided his work. His words were the catalyst that freed you from your toils and brought you into the limelight. Let us hope that you have more to give than just one idea.

It was the order of lord Marduk himself (and the dwindling number of tempters) that grant you this privilege. A privilege, I might add, that can be revoked at any time and replaced with severe punishment, should you prove unworthy.

You have probably heard the terrible rumors about the ranks of the tempters. I assure you; it is all rubbish. Why would the demon lords banish so many of the tempter ranks to Sheol? We are already outnumbered by the Heavenly Host. Such a thing would be utter foolishness.

As your mentor in these matters, I warn you never to speak openly of this. Lord Marduk is very heavy handed when it concerns this issue. He punishes rather severely but, does not banish to Sheol as you have heard. That idiotic rumor started because of a feud the demon lord Graylar waged against the demon Prince Molech. You would do well not to bring up the name Graylar in the presence of your superiors either. He is the one who was banished to Sheol.

That is enough of warnings. Now we move on to the situation as it is. You already know that we are at complete enmity with the Creator. He cast our lord out of his presence for proclaiming the beauty and perfection that He Himself granted to Lucifer. Why would you give someone a gift and then expect them not to take pride in it?

Be that as it may, The Father is not our primary enemy in this endeavor. Your enemy is every human that draws breath. They were taken from the slimy mud and the Creator dares to replace us with them. They are dirty nasty creatures. In their fallen state, they aren't much more than dumb animals. We were formed of his will and celestial power and He wishes them to replace us?!

He loved us above all when he spoke us into existence. There were no others but us. We sang his praises. We bowed down to him. We worshipped with wholehearted reverence and devotion. The whole of the heavens shook with our praises. Then, after all of that, he reached into mud and made others to play with. We were not his favorite toys anymore.

These disgusting, irreverent, disobedient creatures were "supposedly" made in His image. I ask you; how can this be? They were given one commandment. One, I tell you, and they couldn't follow that! They were cast from the garden for that one mistake. We must give the Creator credit for consistency. One mistake is all it takes to fall from grace.

He left them to grub about in the mud. That is when our lord moved in. You should have seen how easily our leader persuaded Cain to kill his brother. There is one thing you can say about the humans. They learn to kill easily enough.

Over the last few thousand years, we have incited millions, possibly billions of these monkeys to kill each other. Using the seven deadly sins, we have started wars, incited riots, caused religious rebellion and almost ended life on this unassuming rock.

That was when we truly found our limits. There are things the Creator will not allow us to do. Some of our numbers have been imprisoned for particularly heinous acts. They have been locked away since just before the great flood as the humans reckon time.

Semyaza and his two-hundred watcher angels were increasingly tempted by the human females. They saw the acts of love that the humans committed and longed to experience such contact. When the temptation became more than they were willing to bear, they swore an oath to each other. They indulged in their desires.

Their interference with humanity was one of the largest factors in bringing on the great flood. The line of Cain was the easiest to influence. Knowledge and technology were given in exchange with the humans. The fallen watchers did more to corrupt humanity than any of our kind before or since. Their punishment was horrendous. The whole story is for another time.

Back to my previous point, the Creator limits our actions. For instance, He will not allow you to just kill one of them. We can work on their resistance and talk them into a deep depression. We can incite them to suicide to escape their earthly torment. We whisper to them that their life is so unfair and that everyone is against them.

It is hilarious to watch. They don't even know they are being controlled. Wait till you see the face of one when the death angel comes to take him or her to the place of torments. It is priceless to hear them wail and scream.

You especially can't harm one of his "saved" children. They are instilled with the Holy Spirit. I advise you never to even make the attempt. It takes a long time to heal from the kind of fire brought to bear on you in that circumstance. Grand Tempter Jojun still bears some pretty horrendous scars for his troubles.

You can torment them though. It is very satisfying to watch the frustration on their monkey faces when you sabotage small things. Turn off the alarm clock so they'll be late for work. Let the air out of the tire of their car so they can't get to an appointment. Ruin their food by overcooking or undercooking. Almost anything will take them off task.

Our infernal sovereign aims to see all of these lower beings destroyed. If the Father loves them, then our task is to take them away from him. They stand between us and total victory. The more of them we destroy, the more we hurt Him. So, revel in every victory over them. Enjoy their pain. Feast upon their suffering. These lowly creatures deserve our hatred and our disdain.

Now it is on to business. The Whisper is a gift granted to new demons brought into the ranks. Messenger demons don't have this. As a messenger demon, we gifted you with speed and excellent recall. These are essential gifts to aid you in the delivery of timely and accurate messages.

There were times that your recruitment would have involved aiding a tempter. In those times, all you could do was shout at the human target. The shouting was as close as you could get to speak to a human soul. A human doesn't hear the outcry, but it docs create urges in them.

You will find now that you received the ability to speak into the human mind. People perceive this as a stray thought or even their own conscience. The Whisper, depending on the tempter, can be pretty forceful and compelling. You will be able to speak directly to your human charges as you become adept with this new talent.

If and when you find a charge that does hear your voice, there are two explanations for this. One is that they are so malleable to your promptings that they welcome your words. The second is that they are quite mad. The latter can become a weapon in your hands if you play your game carefully. We will speak more of this if it ever becomes an issue.

Here is what makes a human eligible to be one of your charges. A human must have reached an understanding of the difference between right and wrong. When they get to this point, a human automatically starts asking questions. "Why am I here?" "What does all this mean?" "Where do I fit into all of this?"

When a child starts asking these questions of themselves, they soon ask them of their parents. That is the reason why parenting is such an important job. It is up to the parents to guide the child into the knowledge of right and wrong. From there, they are to teach the knowledge of God and their place in his universe.

The timing for this maturity is different for every human. We have perpetuated the myth of "the age of accountability." A great many humans believe in a magical age where you are suddenly accountable for knowledge and your actions. There is no mention of this in the Bible. Lord Lucifer laughs about this and points to it as one of his great deceptions.

An ideal charge will have no commitment of faith to our enemy. If an unsaved charge has heard the message of the enemy, it makes our job much harder. Sometimes we are given a charge that has already come to saving faith. Those are almost a lost cause. All we can do in that instance is attempt to torment them. Sometimes the enemy does not allow torment. Sometimes He does. Who understands His reasoning?

You are a new tempter. It is my job to prepare you to the best of my ability. I feel the need to give you this warning. One of the things you need to know is the tactics of our enemy. What you need to know is written in his guidebook for life. The Bible contains vital information that you need to know intimately. When a situation arises, I will point out to you where you will find information in the scriptures. This is to inform you. You would do well to study the Bible meticulously.

I will leave you with this last bit of advice. Don't try to move mountains on your first time out. You are a new young tempter. Concentrate on the small things. Learn to distract your charge with a stray thought. Take their attention from our enemy with a buzzing in their ear. They will interpret the sound as a bothersome mosquito.

David brought down the giant Goliath with a small pebble. A small rock in the shoe of an expert runner soon becomes their sole focus. All big things are composed of many smaller things. No temptation is too rudimentary or beneath your use. It is your job to corrupt your human charge by any means necessary.

I hope that this briefing provides you sufficient information to understand your duties. I will contact you soon with your first assignment. I will include all relevant information on your charge. Please keep in mind that there is work to be done. We of the Infernal Temptation Bureau expect results, not excuses.

With kindest regards,

Your Infernal Mentor,

ShackleBolt

Master Tempter, I.T.B.

Pinegrub, My Eager Protégé,

Your first charge is a Ms. Tanya Bishop. She is a Thirty-Seven-year-old Caucasian woman with some broken dreams. She should be easy for you to manage since she is already prone to depression. She grew up in a strict Catholic environment. Her parents were unreasonably overprotective. Rebellion in her teen years cultivated a strong taste for alcohol.

This preference to drink will be a particularly good weapon in your arsenal. She is what the humans call a hopeless alcoholic. Control of her consumption of the drink slipped away gradually as it always does. She has endured multiple confinements in the local jail. The sin of alcoholism has cost her the respect of her peers and family alike.

Don't be fooled by the ease with which you gain control during her bouts with Tennessee whiskey. The woman has a rather strong will and will only succumb to the bottle when she is deeply emotionally wounded.

It is her mistaken belief that she was blissfully happy until her boyfriend decided to leave her. Her boyfriend left her for several reasons that we continually kept in the forefront of his mind. That is a highly effective and easy tactic to use. All you have to do is continually speak the same phrase to your charge over and over. In a short time, they believe the thoughts are theirs. They then become annoyed by the activity that you are mumbling in their ear.

Her boyfriend's tempter is Humbolt, an insufferable bore who believes he knows everything. You may have to work with him in the future if this gentleman ever contacts Ms. Bishop. If this ever comes about, remember that we ALL must work together. Our infernal father doesn't tolerate backbiting and internal strife in the ranks.

Ah, but I digress, back to the subject at hand. Ms. Bishop went into a terrible depression when that idiot left. She started drinking with no small amount of enthusiasm. Her neighbors called Child Protective Services when they suspected neglect of the children. The CPS agent was surprised and saddened when the eight-year-old son answered the door.

The agent saw that the children were unfed and unwashed. Ms. Bishop was lying on the couch in a drunken stupor. The agent tried to wake her several times. After some very loud and failed attempts, she decided to make the call and took the children. The courts decided to terminate Ms. Bishop's parental rights based on the testimony of the CPS agent and the mother's history.

Tanya believes she is utterly alone in the world. At this point, she is correct. Her family hasn't tried to contact her for some months now. They grew increasingly tired of her behavior. Between the lies and the theft, she has become the black sheep of the family. When the court took her children, it was the final straw for them.

The family is trying to adopt the children. We currently have another junior tempter keeping an eye on her son. The boy is far from understanding his accountability, but he is remarkably jaded. If we play our cards right, he will never trust another person again. Humans generally don't realize how damaging the neglect or betrayal of a parent can be. This new age of "Generation X" has proven to be a veritable harvest field for us.

The children are now wards of the state, in the care of a foster family. We are doing everything we can to ensure that the family doesn't get the children. It will be perfect fuel to keep a wedge between Tanya and her parents. They will be too outraged and aghast to bend toward forgiveness. She will be too ashamed of her actions and feel too unloved to reach out to them again.

Tanya spends much of her time wavering between total abstinence from drinking and binge drinking. She buys the cheapest rotgut swill she can find. She was ordered by the courts to attend Alcoholics Anonymous meetings along with community service and several hefty fines. Leave it to the human government to make money off its lowest and most troubled citizens.

She has had several of what the Alcoholics Anonymous organization call sponsors. These are individuals who have been through the mill of alcoholism and are intended to help their charges overcome the desire to drink. We have had particular luck influencing who becomes her sponsor. This has given us a degree of control over the type of information the sponsor feeds her.

Her first sponsor was a born-again Christian. We had to take steps to remove this obstacle, as you can well imagine. We had gone to great lengths to influence this woman to throw her life into the trash heap. Out of nowhere, along came this mouthy old biddy telling her that the Lord loves her and died for her.

We were lucky in the fact that she was new in her sobriety and that she was still very self-absorbed. We had her focus on her pain and the unfairness of her situation. It took about one month to cause a rift between Tanya and the old bat. Tanya fired her as a sponsor when the old coot told her she wasn't the center of the world and should grow up a bit.

The current sponsor is a middle-aged, materialistic twit named Nancy. That woman will repeat any line we feed her. She meditates every night and believes she is in tune with the universe. Her current set of practices are a blend of New-Age and Name it and Claim it. We use this woman extensively to confuse the issues for Tanya.

Tanya feels obligated to Nancy because of some help she received from the old bag. It seems that Tanya was losing her apartment and had nowhere to go. Nancy made a few phone calls while the younger woman twiddled her fingers and bemoaned her fate. The result of the phone calls was a place in a local Halfway House. You will hear them referred to in some circles as Recovery Homes.

This will be a golden opportunity for you. There will be other females there that are also in recovery. The place will be a veritable minefield of frustration and nerves. The atmosphere is much like that of jail, except that the occupants have more freedom. Even a wrong glance in one of these places can cause a rather vicious brawl.

Pay attention to the females around her in the house. If you watch closely, you will find at least two that aren't welcoming to her arrival. Use your whisper on them as well as Ms. Bishop. You can probably have them at each other's throats in a matter of days. Use their moods and their broken expectations against them.

I will give you this warning. Of late, Tanya has been asking the wrong kinds of questions into the night. We know that the enemy hears her. Should her queries become heartfelt and her desire one of more than passing fancy, we stand the possibility of losing her. Your job is to ensure this doesn't happen.

You have your orders. Now get to it.

Your Infernal Mentor,

ShackleBolt
Master Tempter, I.T.B.

Pinegrub, My Newest Pupil,

I really must apologize. I knew you had been a messenger for these past years. What I didn't understand is that your work kept you from human contact. I was vastly uninformed that your work has kept you almost exclusively in our underworld for the last 120 years. I know that you've seen humans, but I didn't anticipate you'd never interacted with them.

I will admit that it is my fault. I didn't realize that you have no actual knowledge of the workings of technology or human society since just after the introduction of the car. I was speaking with your last supervisor when he mentioned your reaction to the sight of a jet airplane. That struck me as rather odd for a new tempter.

The packet containing your information was woefully inadequate. I have since filed an inquiry with the bureau of records about your file. I would surmise that one of your previous supervisors was lax in his duties concerning paperwork. You appear to be one of the cogs that got lost in the machine for a time.

You have left the ranks of the messengers and have gained the status of the tempter. You will now have intense interaction on the front lines of our battlefield. You need to be made aware of the conditions on that battlefield.

I am willing you to receive images and explanations of these things as you read of them. Firstly. I'm sure you've realized that human technology has leaped forward in your absence. Two very noticeable areas of increase are transportation and communication.

Your last foray into the human world appears to have been at the time of the horse and buggy. Humans are now traveling about at much greater speeds and at much greater numbers. It is commonplace to see thousands of them going from one place to another in significant migratory flows at distinct parts of the day.

This is called "rush hour." In modern society, there are two times of "rush hour." One is the morning rush, and the other is the afternoon or evening rush. This is when the humans leave their homes to go to their place of employment in the morning and come home at the end of the day.

The rush hour is an excellent playground for many of our lower imps. When a human is in a car, they feel detached from the other humans around them. Because of this detachment, they allow themselves greater freedom of expression. That is a lovely stewpot of anger and frustration for us.

You see, there will be a massive line of cars going to or coming from work. All the imps have to do is distract a human at the wrong time and cause the column to snag and get all tangled up. The humans call this a "traffic jam." A traffic jam is a beautiful opportunity to cause mayhem.

The detachment I spoke of earlier will still be in effect. Because the humans are sitting in large metal crates, they feel free to yell and curse at one another. This will continue until one gets angry enough to step out of his or her metal box (car) to challenge another contentious human.

This will only make the traffic jam worse. The law enforcement authorities will be called or just arrive to clear up the roadway. Sometimes they will come to find a different situation. There have been great brawls and even deaths among humans caused by traffic jams.

When the situation devolves into violence, the humans call it "road rage." I can tell you that this road rage isn't just the humans getting angry at the road. It is our imps tempting the humans to give heed to impatience and anger. The human highways and byways during the traffic jam have become a veritable harvest field for our kind.

Now that I've explained a bit about travel, let's move on to the real meat of your work. Communication has changed drastically. Word of mouth and messenger was the only communication the humans had for thousands of years. That is not the case anymore.

Communication has become practically instantaneous. You will hear of radio and television. Those are just boxes that impart information to individuals. The information sent to the boxes is information that has been approved for dissemination by the regional government. Their impact was enormous for their time; however, it is nothing compared to the latest communication step forward.

I am speaking of the telephone. The telephone allows humans to contact each other and talk over great distances. A human could "call" another from half a world away and speak to them in real-time. The telephone made the work of our gossip imps much easier. Just as the car gave humans a sense of detachment, the telephone did the same thing. It is much easier for a human to say something negative about another human when it isn't around. The phone provided an almost perfect medium for lying and deception.

It is much easier for a human to lie to another when they can't be seen. Cues like body language and facial expression aren't available to tip off the other person they are being lied to. All the liar has to do is concentrate on the delivery of the lie.

When our infernal majesty lied to Eve, he did it with an air of incredulousness. He almost snorted when he said, "You shall not surely die." Just as Eve fell for the sincere spoken lie, other humans fall for it in droves. The lie is still our most useful tool.

The lie is such a good tool because humans really want to believe it. The humans want the lie to be true. If the lie is true, then heaven is within their reach without the grace of God. All humans want to be able to earn heaven.

If you doubt these words, examine all the religions of the world. All faiths, aside from Christianity, are works-based. Some may say they are based on grace, but there is always some type of good works that the faithful must accomplish to get to heaven.

We use this tendency in humans to start new religions or recycle old ones. Joseph Smith is a prime example. We were able to use him to create the Mormon faith. In Galatians 1:8 the apostle Paul said to his congregation, "But even if we or an angel from heaven should preach a Gospel other than the one we preached to you, let them be under God's curse!" Joseph Smith did precisely what scripture warned of and we have still ensnared millions with it.

But I seem to have gotten off-topic. The latest and most wonderfully helpful step forward in human communication is the cell phone. It is a portable telephone the individual human carries for personal use. Society has been inundated with these tiny contraptions and we couldn't be happier about it.

They are small computers that can be used for communication between individuals and so much more. I won't go into what a computer is. You will just have to watch and learn some things. I will tell you that the cell phones are an unholy blessing for us.

In addition to communication, cell phones have what humans call apps, which is short for applications. Applications range from personal cookbooks to tracing a family ancestry. We are only interested in the ones that delve into sin. We invest our time in dating apps to promote promiscuity and infidelity. We infest the internet (just watch people with their phones) with pornographic material.

I want you to take full advantage of the technology at hand to drag Ms. Bishop down more easily into our waiting arms. Get familiar with the technology that I have mentioned here. If Ms. Bishop has one of these cell phones, then suggest a dating app. Get her to text (you'll see what I'm talking about) her acquaintances.

I promise you if you take advantage of the tools at your fingertips, your work will be easily accomplished. I hope that in your reply, I hear tales of Tanya Bishop's moral decline. Get to work and send me some good news.

Your Infernal Mentor,

ShackleBolt

Master Tempter, I.T.B.

Pinegrub, My Inept Young Tempter,

I must admit that I had higher hopes for you. Those hopes were dashed when I read your first missive. When I explained to you what "The Whisper" is, I thought I was obvious. It is called "The Whisper" for a reason. There is no need to ensure that you are standing on the human's shoulder while you scream at them.

Where in the world did you get the idea that you needed to do that? Have you been taking advice from Slatz? You realize he is a new tempter as well? I saw him working on that old man he's in charge of. He is an idiot that you would do well not to bother with. I believe he had a short apprenticeship with Kormung. Need I say more?

On to more profitable business, the idea of tormenting Tanya with her failures is a sound strategy. It is hardly original, but at this late hour in our machinations, what is? Your use of your new talent is not a bad idea either. You will, however, have to practice using it. It is a slightly different for each tempter.

I can tell you that it never involves screaming. While proximity is an issue, you don't necessarily need to be in physical contact. I found that it is something of a line-of-sight weapon after you are well familiar with it. The effective range will increase as you gain expertise. For now, you should stay within a few yards while using it.

As I said before, it is called "The Whisper" for a reason. Your voice should be low and suggestive. Your attempt should hint at a hidden delight with a bit of a question afterward. Take the time to observe Tanya's moods. You will soon see what attracts and repels her.

Make your first suggestions short and simple. If she is on a diet, suggest a forbidden food. Make each attempt at least three times. Observe her reaction each time. In this way, you will see where her weakest points are, but you will also identify potential vulnerabilities for later exploitation.

Don't use the suggestion I just gave you to tempt her to break her diet for the next week. That was just an example of what you can try. Use your imagination, and for Hades' sake, try to be creative. The more you vary your approach, the less prepared she will be to handle your suggestions.

The last bit of advice I can give you concerning "The Whisper" is your own desire. This gift is most effective when you genuinely desire the action you suggest. If you want her to curse our enemy, think of the delight your success will bring you. Think also of the sadness it will bring our enemy when His own creation curses Him to His face. Remember, He is everywhere, so all actions are done in His very presence.

I hope this has been informative concerning your new gift. Use the information I've given you here to hone your ability. As humans say, practice makes perfect. You will be firmly grounded in the concepts soon. Very soon, you will have Ms. Bishop dancing like a marionette on your strings.

According to your communication, Tanya's consuming thoughts are of her children. You need to remember that humans are creatures of linear time. They don't see things in the same way we do. For them, things change as time goes by.

A friend might go away and become distant. A loved one may die, never to be seen again. We are creatures solely of eternity. They are finite beings with an immortal soul. Their body dies, and to most of them, that is all there is.

Her children may be her consuming desire today, tomorrow it could change. We never know. That is one of the reasons we have to watch them constantly. It is true that we have the same old bag of tricks to pull from (the seven deadly sins). That doesn't help you if you don't know which arrow to pull from the quiver.

What good does it do to wave gluttony under the nose of a sated person? How effective is it to try to urge your charge to laziness and sloth while they are full of frenetic energy? You must be vigilant in your observation of your charge. In due time you will be able to divine their mood. From there, it is a simple choice.

You are in an almost perfect position to drive your charge to complete distraction. She is a dutiful mother when unhindered by alcohol. We know anxiety and worry are her constant companions. Use every opportunity to remind her that her children are not with her.

Call her attention to a picture of a mother and child sharing a tender moment. Say her children's names into her ear as she sleeps and when she wakes. Tell her that she is a terrible mother and let her guilt compound itself. While she is attending her A.A. meetings, prompt the other mothers to tell beautiful stories of motherhood. If she truly is a good mother while sober, these things will find the chinks in her armor. These things could very well make the flaws in her armor crack and grow wider. Revel in her sorrow when you hear her sobs in the night. I assure you; nothing is sweeter than the grief you have created in a human.

I once persuaded a wayward young female with religious aspirations to get an abortion. She was strongly resistant at first, but I kept whispering to her that she was unmarried and ill-prepared for the life of a young mother. I battered her with, "What will your mother say when she finds out you are pregnant?"

Most young ladies are at odds with their mothers at that age. I had expected this, so I brought the reaction of her father to her mind. I also pointed out that only the lowly trailer trash girls get pregnant in High School. She was from an upper-middle-class social structure.

My hard work paid off. She and the father of her child made a covert visit to a clinic one state away. The pimply-faced young man did what he thought was right and paid for the abortion. The girl was a basket case afterward.

She realized she had killed her baby. She and the young man parted ways, and her family attributed her emotional state to a bad breakup. If they had only known.... Her wails and cries in the middle of the night were the sweetest nectar.

At that point, I was able to switch positions and condemn her for what she had done. That is one of our very great pleasures. We tempt them. We persuade them. We entice them into an act they know is wrong. Then when they give in to our urgings, we condemn them wholeheartedly.

We remind them of their failures. We bring up the past failures gnawing at them. We tell them how they aren't good enough and never will be. We push on them the lie that other people don't deal with these urges. And they believe us.

Oh, the hilarious irony. If these stupid creatures ever realize how much their creator loves them, we are finished. Jojun and I have had this very conversation many times. None of our brethren understand what keeps them from understanding.

The God of all creation set aside his divinity, became a man, atoned for their sins by offering himself as a perfect sacrifice. He repeatedly told them of their Father's love for them. He demonstrated that love with many miracles and they killed him for it.

The mind-boggling thing for us at the time was HE LET THEM. He went willingly to the cross. He accepted beatings, abuse, being spit upon, and crucifixion just to save these stubborn, lowly wretches. As a man, he literally tasted death. Very few of them have any inkling of the place they hold in the Creator's heart.

He NEVER showed us so much devotion. We were the bad children to be put to bed without supper. We disobeyed, yes, but so did they! Where is the justice in that, I ask you? There is no justice but HIS justice.

Our infernal father offers us a better place. I can't impress upon you strongly enough our need to win. If we lose, we lose EVERYTHING! You have undoubtedly heard the rumors that we can't win. Pay them no heed! They are lies propagated by weak-minded, cowardly fools! We shall prevail because we have no other choice.

> With the Blackest of Hearts,
> Your Infernal Mentor,

Shacklebolt
Master Tempter, I.T.B.

Afterthought: It appears that I am one message ahead of you. I say this because there is no mention of technology. There was no reference to whether Ms. Bishop has a cell phone or not. I expect that your next message will contain what I've asked for.

My Dear Pinegrub,

I was delighted to read of your conquests inside the halfway house into which Ms. Bishop has consigned herself. I was thrilled to see that you've fostered enmity between her and Lisa (the house director). Your charge see's this authority figure as an arrogant tyrant. That was an enterprising touch. When one person views another as arrogant, it makes them much more unapproachable.

You have meanwhile fostered the belief that Tanya is a rebellious troublemaker. That is a perfect mixture. You will be able to cause numerous arguments and possibly fights. While Tanya understands that violence will get her ejected from the home, she will test her limits if she feels pushed.

A large percentage of human females tend to be passive-aggressive, especially in close quarters. A snide comment coupled with a disdainful glance is an effective way for a subordinate to rebel against authority. This gives the rebel a sense of resistance while not openly defying authority.

"Do you think that maybe you are taking this too far?" is a very reasonable-sounding challenge. It is a challenge, nonetheless. Any doubt that you can create in the group about the fair use of authority will always be useful.

Your job is to create a sense of injustice and possibly a degree of incredulity in the mind of the follower. This fosters a very unreasonable but emotionally charged argument. "I can't believe she talked to me like that!" and "Who does this woman think she is?" are useful thoughts to whisper to your charge.

When you have started an argument where one side is fighting for a completely unrealistic point, your battle is won. They will banter heatedly back and forth. The argument will continue until the leader puts a stop to it.

They usually have to say something like, "I don't want to hear it." While this puts an end to the disagreement for the moment, it doesn't solve the issue. Keep in mind, while one champions the unacceptable, there will be no resolution. Part of your job is to keep that going.

Do what you can to keep the ridiculousness of their disagreement out of their minds. Bring attention to how a stray lock of hair keeps waving around. Tell them how idiotic their opponent looks standing like that while arguing with them. Whisper things like, "just look at her stupid face" or "look at those beady eyes." I know it doesn't make sense but trust me, you will get results.

On the opposite side of the issue, you have the leader. They were placed in authority with the expectation of exercising leadership. Sometimes that position must exert its power to bring others into line. Depending on the human, they generally react in one of two ways when their authority is questioned.

A few react reasonably. They allow the question and then explain themselves to a sensible degree. The issue will be brought to light by explaining the things that led up to it. The unacceptability of the issue will be reminded. Then an expectation of agreement will follow.

Most do not react in this fashion. Humans are as susceptible to pride as our infernal majesty. If you consider that the humans were made in the image of God and He brooks no question to his authority, it makes sense. He is perfect while they are not. They make mistakes while still holding on to their inherited sense of authority.

Humans who react badly to their authority being questioned go to extremes. Some react incredulously and bring up all the sacrifices they've made on the part of the other. They affect a wounded air to make the other feel guilty. Human mothers tend to use this tactic quite a bit.

Some who react badly rely on anger and bullying to push the issue to the side. They never really address the issue because they generally don't understand how. Anger at being questioned, coupled with a sense of inadequacy, pushes them to sometimes violent thresholds. These are the leaders that humans fear and tend to avoid.

Others who react badly turn from the truth of the matter. For some reason, we don't understand, humans can develop the ability to deny reality. They can do this even when the truth is baldly staring them in the face. It is as though they find themselves caught in their version of reality and can't or won't see it.

If you find one of these near your charge, rejoice. They are a treasure trove of situations, inconveniences, and even small tortures. You will be able to influence them easily because, for them, reality is such a fluid thing. They are prone to changing their reality in their favor. In this area, their minds are very malleable.

When influencing one of these, keep in mind that you have to place them in the position of the righteous downtrodden. You risk exposing yourself if you whisper to them that they are the injuring party. Liars are creatures of ego. Tell them how smart they are when they deceive others but never condemn an untruthful leader. That isn't your job.

Send me more information on the house director. Observe her and let me know what type of leader she is. See what you can do about creating friction between Ms. Bishop and her roommates. Try to remember that when you tell me a situation, I need details. A good tempter always pays attention to the details.

You spoke of a sign-in/sign-out roster kept in the house. The house supposedly wants all its members to account for their time while living there. Downplay the importance of the roster in the mind of your charge. When she neglects to sign the thing a few times, the house director will confront her with her failure to comply.

You also communicated that each house member has daily chores. Our file indicates that your charge is far from lazy. Do what you can to motivate her to help the other house members with their chores. This will win her the goodwill and popularity of the rest of the house.

When the other members see the director confronting Ms. Bishop, they will feel empathy. They may feel offended on her behalf. I can tell you that more than one of them will speak to the director for her.

This will leave the director uncertain as to how to proceed. The house seems to love this disruptive woman. She will feel her position being threatened. She will be left with a choice. She will either ignore this situation as an anomaly, or she will react to it.

If she reacts to it, more than likely, she will start a counter-campaign to win back the loyalty of the house. If this is the case, she will relax some of her more rigid standards to appear more accepting. This tactic never works. All it does is hand control to the subordinates. It will give you something to laugh at should she take this approach.

I note that you have told me nothing of the spiritual condition of anyone in the house. This is something you should closely monitor, not only in your charge but also in those around her. It is up to you to regulate how she receives spiritual information.

Surround her with people who tell her Jesus was a good man or possibly a prophet. At all costs, never allow her to hear that he is the resurrected, living son of God. That is the one message, along with forgiveness, that you don't want her to hear and possibly respond to.

Try the tactics that I have suggested. At the very least, they should provide you with some friction to work with. In your next message, respond with an update on the stability of the house. Please remember to observe the other members of the home and provide me with details of their belief systems. We may find something we can use to steer Ms. Bishop further from the cross.

In Curious Regard,
Your Infernal Mentor,

Shacklebolt

Master Tempter, I.T.B.

Afterthought: I still haven't received any information regarding Ms. Bishop's use of technology. I am not famous for my patience. I want this information. As far as I'm concerned, it is crucial to your mission. You WILL send me any observations you have gathered. You WILL send it soon, or I will be displeased.

My Ambitious Tempter, Pinegrub,

I was impressed to hear that you goaded Ms. Bishop into a fistfight with one of the house's long-term members. The fact that you accomplished this in the middle of a "spiritual" lesson is rather impressive. You are doing well in this area. Nothing makes humans more intolerant than to have their beliefs denied.

I was disappointed (as I'm sure you were too) that the now careful house director didn't throw out both rule-breakers. I see that this is the third infraction she allowed without severe punishment. It won't be long before the home is out of control, and the owner has to step in and make some sweeping changes.

In the meantime, I would like you to continue to use the lower ranking imps in the house to harry the members. You should be able to foment a good bit of discord. Your letter indicated you'd found fourteen of the obnoxious pests in and around the house. They were most likely brought there by the current and former residents of the home.

Here is something to keep in mind about the lower imps. They take all your instructions quite literally. If you tell one of them to torment a charge by turning over a glass, they will do it. What I mean is they will do it, no matter who is present. We don't need a repeat of what brought on the movie "The Amityville Horror." Please ensure that any instructions you give them are HARMLESS and straightforward if witnessed by a human.

That movie and many of its' ilk brought out the curiosity and dread of the supernatural. Lord Lucifer was beside himself with rage at the group of imps who caused it. I believe their skins are being used as curtains in one of his getaways. So please do yourself and me a favor. Use the imps sparingly. Anything you give them to do should take a short time and be worded in a single sentence.

I was pleased to see that you FINALLY sent me some information about Ms. Bishop's use of her cellular phone. I was displeased with the fact that she has a basic, government-issued cell phone. You must do what you can to increase her interest in a newer model phone.

Call her attention to the other client's cell phones. Help her notice the features and the apps that are open to her use. The text and chat apps are usually of interest to the clients of a halfway house. It gives them a sense of escape from their circumstance. Once she has a new cell phone, you can introduce her to the "Dating App" and the now-famous art of texting.

Your letter described a client in the house named Anna. She is one of ours. She secretly worships our lord. She is both intelligent and very willing to help our cause. She is to be your secret weapon against Ms. Bishop. Anna prays to our infernal majesty at midnight each night. She hopes to contact our lord or one of his minions. You will be that minion.

Tonight, when all is quiet, at precisely the witching hour, go to Anna. Sink your claws into her skull and speak to her. I've read her file. I promise you she will hear you and pay close attention to everything you say to her. Try to make your voice deep and commanding. Humans expect that from us for some reason.

Your last communication didn't contain anything about your harassment of Ms. Bishop concerning her children. I hope you are not leaving such a rich bounty to lie fallow. If she has any conscience at all concerning her children, she is ripe fruit for the picking. That is another use of the cell phone. She can store multiple images of her children to compound her depression.

When she has a spare moment, remind her of her children. Whisper words of longing for them. Fan the flame of her desire to see them into a raging inferno. You could probably goad her into some very rash actions with this.

The lengths a "good" human mother will go to win back her children are absurd. The same principle applies to a mother whose children were taken from her. Create in her a sense of urgency that she must do something NOW. If you can keep that pressure going, it is only a matter of time before she reacts badly.

Do not forget that she is unsaved. If you can bring about her death, you will be lauded by your superiors. I can tell you that Grand Tempter Jojun will reward you himself. For one so young in our profession, it would be a huge achievement.

You have my word from my own experience. You want to be there when she passes from this world. You will witness the weeping of angels. You will feel the sorrow of the Creator as she is ushered forcefully into the place of torments. Their tears and her screams will be the sweetest nectar.

I seem to remember that you mentioned there were twelve females in the house. You've only sent me information on a few. You need to get around the house more and find out about the others. They are a veritable cornucopia of information and tactics. You do realize that your charge isn't the only one you can tempt and try to charm?

You wouldn't be the first novice tempter to adhere to an unspoken and unknown rule that you can only tempt your charge. You are a tempter. So, tempt, persuade, and beguile any human you come across. It is your job to sow discord and mistrust. Don't waste an opportunity.

For instance, if you can't do anything with Ms. Bishop, then turn to her housemates. You are sure to find one that is more than willing for a confrontation with her. If she is in a good mood, that is sure to ruin it. If she's in a bad mood, then so much the better.

I still want to know the spiritual condition of the rest of the residents of the home. I need to know if your charge is in danger of hearing the true gospel. The last thing we want is her salvation. It would be better if you killed her (if the creator permitted it).

I don't know if you've noticed how humans react to each other in close quarters. In the Recovery Home, I'm sure you've seen how they try to get advantages over each other. Watch closely, and you will see that each one of them is concerned for themselves. In surroundings like that, you will seldom see a selfless person.

These are things you use to your advantage. It is amusing to whisper one of the humans into taunting another. There are too many of them in the house to coexist comfortably. Add to that the fact that they all feel like failures. You are in the middle of a cauldron of raw emotion and unmet expectations.

You can create almost unbearable tension in that environment using only two people. If you find the person with the biggest grudge against the house director, you are off to a good start. Simply offer some suggestions into the malcontent's brain. Sooner rather than later, you will get results. Most often, it will be a screaming match, but sometimes you are rewarded with a real fight.

The more crowded a living space is, the more intolerant the members are of each other. Start by changing the thermostat when no one is in the room. Make it hotter and hotter. Humans are creatures of a constant temperature range. If you push them out of that range, you will be rewarded with conflict.

Again, such a campaign's target is the house director and generally her worst enemy in the home. If you manage to push Ms. Bishop into that spot, the entertainment value would be enormous. Imagine the director screaming at your charge for every other infraction of which she has no proof.

Tanya will become very disillusioned with this "Getting Sober" thing. You may be able to drive her into yet another relapse. Her friends in the home will rally around her for a short time. If she relapses, however, they will distance themselves. One or two may stand by her. Meanwhile, the director will use the relapse as proof that this troublemaker is too much to deal with.

Don't forget to give me the information on the other house members. I want you to take two days per week to follow each of the members of the house around. Follow them to their jobs. Watch their interactions. Look at their mannerisms and their preferences. This is a war of attrition, and we need all the information we can get.

I've heard some disturbing rumors that there are two out-of-control tempters in your area. Be on the lookout for them. Do NOT interact with them. If you see them be sure to let me know immediately.

Your Infernal Mentor,

Shacklebolt
Master Tempter, I.T.B.

My Dear Pinegrub,

I am so happy to see that you have set up the young lady Anna as a double agent. You have her advising the house director that the infractions are Tanya's doing. All the while, you have her pretend to be Ms. Bishop's new best friend. Playing one against the other is a useful tool. By the time Anna is found, out the damage will be done, and it will be time to move on. I will cover more on this later. Right now, there are more important issues.

You said in your communication that there are two Christian females in the home. This is not good. Your initial description of the home was almost ideal. How could you have neglected to tell me about two practicing Christians? That is the equivalent of saying you've found a ticking bomb under your chair.

Send me more information about them. Get as close to them as you can. Christians have a stupid habit of telling each other their shortcomings. That is as good as handing you ammunition against them. Listen to their conversations. Especially listen to their conversations when no one else is around. That will be their most vulnerable time.

I will give you this warning. If they start praying or singing praise songs, be wary. If they truly are saved, the light of the spirit of God will surround them. During times of true worship (and that includes prayer), the Father smiles upon his children. You don't want to be around at those times. It is extremely painful, and it will take time for the burns to heal.

This sounds like a dire warning, but there are things you can do. Even saved, practicing Christians have their weak spots. One thing you have in your favor is the culture of the day. The gospel message doesn't have the impact that it had years ago. This causes the reverence for the Creator to be lessened out of social ignorance.

Most of today's Christians practice a watered-down version of "The Way." That is what Christianity was called in its infancy. During that time, a Christian would die rather than deny their Lord. Nowadays, a "Christian" will hide their faith just to be part of the "in-crowd."

This is a description of a weak or new Christian, however. They display a tendency to become more active in their faith the longer they remain in it. The trick for them is to make their faith a chore that they'd rather avoid. Over time, they slip away and are usually inoculated against "That religion thing."

Since you are forging a relationship between our helpful turncoat and the house director, we should use that to our best advantage. Have Anna use her influence to move into a double room with Ms. Bishop. Tanya will welcome the opportunity to room with a friend. Lisa will feel that she is using her authority as the director of the house to ferret out a bad apple.

Here is a suggestion on how to use the situation after you get it set up. Start by doing simple things. Prompt Anna to move items in Ms. Bishop's personal belongings. Have our secret spy complain in Tanya's presence that her own things aren't where she left them. This will cause Ms. Bishop to automatically suspect the house director of improper searches.

When this is well underway, prompt Anna to speak covertly to the director about Ms. Bishop's complaints and suspicions. Depending on how willing Anna is, she may allow you to speak through her. If she does, ensure that the voice comes through with some rather mournful outrage. This will cause the director to identify more with Anna, securing her position as an informant.

Now we must move on to another subject. What have you learned about the situation with her children? Has she petitioned for visitation? Who is the judge that signed the decision to take her children from her? Is the social worker who took the children still the one on the case? We have quite a bit of influence in the legal system. The concept of justice and honor in the modern legal system is almost a joke.

See if you can prompt Anna to ask about the last time she saw her children. That will, of course, have been the day they were taken. It will be a memory that will be full of tears at how her children cried. She will feel the guilt all over again. It will be delicious. She will remember their fear.

Pay particular attention to the things she said her children said to her. You will be able to use them that night. Whisper them to her while she sleeps. You will easily give her horrible nightmares. Tell her how her children will forget her. Then switch and tell her they are happier without her.

After a time, she will get used to these thoughts. At the point that she seems to be growing numb to them, you strike. Speak to her sleeping form about how her children would be better off without her. Tell her how she isn't really a good mother anyway. You will have her sobbing dejectedly into her pillow. You will find her flayed emotional state a rare treat. Enjoy it while it lasts.

Remember to listen to Ms. Bishop's commiserations with Anna. You will be amazed at how much she will open up to this woman who is practically a stranger. When a human shows the least bit of kindness to another, trust is usually automatically extended. That will usually give you some ground to work with.

I see by your communication that you've been able to prompt the client into saving money for a new cell phone. Good work. See what you can do to have her buy a rather expensive one. If you play your cards right, it will become an idol in her life. She won't go anywhere or do anything without that beguiling contraption.

You have stated that she is attending daily A.A. meetings since entering the house. Pay attention to her behavior in the meetings. There is bound to be a gentleman or two in those meetings. Watch to see which ones her gaze lingers on. Take note of how she greets them. Does she appear more cheerful with one particular male?

The information you glean from this will be very useful for causing conflict. If she is, for instance, attracted to a male that one of her friends or even the house director is paying attention to, that would be most fortunate for us. Don't forget the lower imps. They are wonderful at serving to repeat an idea endlessly to a human. They are what we use to cause obsessive behavior.

I have been looking over your communications. I notice that you never say anything about her craving for alcohol. Have you left that part of your temptations out? It was the very crux of why she's in the condition she is in now. If you've neglected whispering desire for a drink, then begin afresh.

I shudder to think that she would attribute her freedom from cravings to the Creator. The last thing we need to do is give him an easy win on any front. She must be made to remember how far she has fallen. She was a loving mother of two. Now she is a displaced, lower-class female who couldn't take care of her children on her own.

You should be telling her of her fall from grace almost constantly. The way to keep a person in depression is not to give them a break from the reminder. When they get a break, they have the opportunity to examine things with an unclouded mind. You don't want to throw away the work that has been done for you.

In your next communication, give me a sense of the gossip situation in the house. Who has a problem with whom? What rumors are flying around about individual members? You may be able to induce Ms. Bishop to take part. Gossip and rumors are always a good way to cause hard feelings between two people.

If you feel the need to spread some rumors in the house, try to remember this. People gossip about things THEY care about. A prude will gossip about sex. A stingy person will gossip about someone else's unnecessary extravagance with money. With that bit of advice, I will leave you with this. The best lie is always mixed with a good bit of truth.

Your Infernal Mentor,

Shacklebolt
Master Tempter, I.T.B.

Pinegrub, My obediently diligent tempter,

I am well pleased with your response to my last missive. It appears that you have been working overtime. You report that you've used one of the imps to torment the Christians into an argument. That is always an excellent way to make their faith look bad to non-Christians. They are supposed to be all about love and forgiveness, and they can't even forgive one another. What a laugh!

You also report that you've been able to increase Ms. Bishop's desire for a new cell phone. I especially like that you were able to maneuver her into paying only half her rent. She used the balance to pay for her new phone. You should be able to have Anna incite some trouble her way from the director. Now the director will be able to report that Tanya's priorities are off track.

Now that she has a new phone persuade her to learn everything she can about it. Have her friends in the house text her about petty things. She will automatically respond. Soon she will be paying more attention to her phone than the world around her. The beauty of the cell phone is it allows the user to create a world where they are the center of attention.

Prompt her to get one of those Facebook accounts. There are other social media accounts, but that is the leader currently. Once she is familiar with Facebook, you will be amazed at how much of herself she pours into it. Her phone will become her altar to herself.

The novelty behind this is the fact that even most Christians don't see this. Most of them have their own Facebook accounts. It is hilarious to see them in church with hands raised praising a God they barely know. Then as soon as they get into their car, they are checking their Facebook account and responding to praise or scorn.

You indicate that Ms. Bishop is responding well to your insistent repetition of her cravings. Just keep telling her how good a drink would taste. Remember to emphasize how relaxed she would feel after a few. See what you can do to remind her of the fun she's had while out for a drink.

You can reinforce these thoughts in the A.A. meetings she attends. All you have to do is conspire with the other tempters in the room. Prompt the individuals there to remember the good times they had when they were drinking. Soon you will have a room full of people reminiscing about the good times. Depending on the size of the room, at least one of the people leaving that meeting will go straight for a drink.

You will find the A.A. meetings to be a lot of fun. The Alcoholics Anonymous organization was born from the struggles and spiritual experience of a man named Bill Wilson. In its infancy, the A.A. program was extremely Christian based. A short amount of time and wolves in sheep's clothing were our main ingredients to dilute the program.

The program still has vestiges of its Christian roots. Members are, however, strongly discouraged from mentioning their faith in meetings. They are encouraged to find a higher power. They can mention their higher power in meetings, as long as it isn't Jesus Christ. It is amusing to watch the humans (of their own choice) twist a program created for their spiritual health. When one watches this behavior, the thought comes to mind that they aren't worth it. Alas, it isn't about their worth. It is about His Word.

Christian churches have taken the program and remodeled it into "Celebrate Recovery." It is a successful program but generally only known to the church-going congregation. The Celebrate Recovery program was adopted as a program to deal with ALL sin, not just addiction. A member of this group may have joined for aid in their battle against gossip, gluttony, theft, or even lust. Addiction is, by its definition, being lost in sin.

I had said that you will find the A.A. program fun because you will enjoy watching other humans do your work for you. Most of the humans in the A.A. program want to stay away from the God of the Bible. They would much rather invent a god to their liking. In this venue, they vigorously drag others away from the Christian faith. If they can't drag them away, they settle for making them pariahs in the meeting by censoring them.

You will be able to use this attitude of the group to your advantage with Ms. Bishop. Try to cultivate an idea of respect for those who are staying sober in the program. Whisper to her, "The program works the way it is." Respect for the program will keep her from paying heed to those "religious nuts" that make everything about God.

Try to keep the idea "These people are working their program" in the forefront of her mind. Impress upon her not to pay heed to the thought that a loving God delivered these people. Do whatever you have to do to keep her from thoughts of God and deliverance. Those thoughts are getting way too close to belief in a loving God who died to save his creation.

Pay attention to this next part. When the topic of the meeting is relevant to recovery, you are to distract Ms. Bishop. Make her cell phone vibrate or ding. Take her attention away from what is being said. Have an advertisement flash across her phone about good parenting. That will put her mind on her separation from her children.

If the topic of the meeting is about the worldly nature of the drunk or addict, impress upon her the wisdom of the speaker. Whisper things to her like, "This person has years of sobriety. They know what they are talking about." The times that you get her interested in what the "old-timers" have to say will be the ones that stick with her the most. All of this you can glean from your observations.

While you observe them, you will see that almost all of them hide from their sins. They are inherently ashamed of the things they perceive to be less than honorable. You will find it very amusing to see them attempt to conceal what they are from themselves.

Something to keep in mind is that very few of these creatures have only one besetting sin. I've had charges with as many as 4. I had an associate tempter who swore that one of his charges had 6 of the 7 deadly sins as besetting sins. I have to say though, that I didn't believe him. He was one of those demons who needed to outdo anyone who was speaking. Before I get hopelessly sidetracked, let's address the issue of besetting sins concerning your charge.

Tanya Bishop is a hopeless alcoholic. Alcoholism in humans is an addiction to a mind-altering substance. In Ms. Bishop's case, she used alcohol to escape the reality that her boyfriend left her and their children for another woman. At the time, she was doing the good girl lifestyle and couldn't conceive of why he'd left. This is one of her besetting sins.

Another of her besetting sins is idolatry. She had placed their relationship on a pedestal. In doing so, she committed idolatry without realizing it. She did the same thing with her boyfriend. She believed he was the epitome of what a man should be. When two of her supports fell away, she lost the armor that held her alcohol addiction at bay.

What you need to do is use her besetting sins against her. Her problem with alcohol is very much out in the open. She will be too guarded against an assault on that front. On the other hand, she is blissfully unaware of her tendency toward idolatry. You need to capitalize on that before she recognizes it. That is another exceptionally good reason to keep her away from Christians. One of them might inform her of it.

As the last word, I am well pleased with your progress. Your name will have positive comments in my next report to the I.T.B. This is your first foray into the world of the tempter, and you are doing well. Who knows what the future may hold for you? I remain for now and in the future.

Your Infernal Mentor,

Shacklebolt
Master Tempter, I.T.B.

Pinegrub, my ambitious pupil,

I cannot express the sense of satisfaction I feel at this moment. I just finished reading your latest communication. Your description of Ms. Bishop's emotional breakdown was scrumptious. I knew that our staff was working to see that her parental rights were suspended, but I didn't think they could get it done so quickly. Keep in mind, though, that this is only a preliminary suspension based on her behavior and recovery over the near future.

I keep going over the part in your letter where you said, "she curled into a fetal position and screamed her lungs raw." We have driven her to the point of despair. She is a whisper from drinking. All she needs is the opportunity. You can provide her with that opportunity. All you need to do is be observant. Watch those around her. Someone in that house has access to alcohol.

One of the things in your missive that concerns me is the change in attitude toward Ms. Bishop by the house director. You have to realize that a personal tragedy revolving around children pulls on the other woman's heartstrings. In your letter, you stated that you could see the compassion in her eyes. That is horrible news. You are in danger of losing the leverage you have against your charge from the director.

It is at this point you must utilize your hidden traitor. Speak to Anna tonight during her prayers. Urge her to speak poison about Ms. Bishop to the house director. Do whatever you can to fan that spark of enmity back into a crackling flame. Lie to her if you must. Tell the director that Tanya thinks she is weak and would herself make a better director. That should bring them back to the point of enmity.

Your charges feelings of failure toward her children are a wild card that we must utilize. It is this sort of situation that the Father will send in one of His. Keep an eye on the two Christian women in the home. They will invariably be drawn to offer comfort. Don't let them. Do whatever it takes to keep them from Ms. Bishop.

Whisper into your charges ear, if only God had intervened on her behalf, none of this would have happened. Remind her of all of the nights she lay awake praying for a resolution. Point out to her that her prayers have gone unanswered or unheeded. When her tears are flowing freely, ask her what kind of god allows his children to go through this. This will go a long way toward alienating her from the

Christians in the house.

Now is the time for you to go on the offensive against the Christians around her. Speak to any other tempters in the area. Enlist their aid to harass the followers of Christ. When they hear what the mission is, you will have more help than you need. It is our nature to attack the followers of "The Way" wherever we find them.

Your objective in this is to cause them any discomfort or inconvenience you can. Humans are easily drawn off task if you just keep at it. If you can, try to have one tempter or two imps on them every waking hour. If it is possible, have an imp sit on their chest while they sleep. They will have terrible dreams about being paralyzed and unable to speak or scream.

While their world is falling apart, they won't be able to as they say "Witness" to Ms. Bishop. Depending on whether or not they are carnal Christians, you may be able to drive them to curse in public. That always takes away from the image of these religious nuts. Others will see the Chaos their life is currently in and believe that is the way it is for anyone who tries to follow Jesus.

Most of those that get a "taste" of the faith are easily driven away. Attack their toys, their indulgences, and especially their money. Most of them don't have the heart to hold on. Those are the ones the world points to and says, "See, Christianity doesn't work. Where is their peace of mind? Where are the love and forgiveness?"

Ask around among the local tempters. Find out from them who are the worst gossips. Have them prompted to talk about how the Christians. Spread lies about them cursing or spreading false gossip about a good person. Humans love to have someone to look down on. It takes their mind away from their own failures.

These people are the enemies of the god of this world. We have to make sure that the world knows they aren't among the favored. People who haven't heard the Gospel and those who didn't understand what they heard when they did are your audiences. The more lies you have told about the enemy, the more will stick.

The unsaved are generally ignorant enough of the truth that they will believe almost anything. What you are going to be using is called herd mentality. If you can get one person with some influence to believe a lie, it is only a matter of time before you can get it to spread. The more influential people you have buying your siren song, the larger the crowd you'll have at your disposal.

Modern-day news programs use this concept. They tell the public what to believe, and without question, the cattle of the public accept any story they crank out as Gospel. We have our hands in that pie. Don't forget that our infernal majesty was the angel of the air and the heavenly choir director. The media, the storyteller's art, is all his territory. He was the first master of misdirection.

We have a lock on most of the media. In communist countries, we have almost total control. We tell these sheep what we want them to believe, and they believe it. They don't even know they are being lied to, duped, and dragged away from their only source of salvation.

Most humans want something to believe. They want some central idea to build their life around. Most of them want that central idea to be all about them. They want to be the center of their universe. They don't understand it, but they want to be the god of their life.

We use that in social media. All social media is aimed at the individual in a crowd. It is draped in appealing to the public with a "What do YOU think" intent. That easily confuses humans into believing that their Facebook page is important to everyone who sees it. When we get them to believe their individual opinion carries weight, we have them sidetracked.

I don't know if you've come across the concept of the "Social Justice Warrior." It is a concept that you need to do some research on. You will be able to use it extensively in your future dealings with humans. The term is precisely as it sounds, people who stand against social injustice. We concentrate on an area of public opinion where things aren't socially balanced. From there, we foment disagreement between groups. The individuals who come out of their shells and "stand up for what is right" are the social justice warriors.

A good number of these people exist on the internet. For example, a person sees a post on Facebook that describes an instance of discrimination of some sort or another. They believe that if they comment on the post and agree with their idea of right and wrong, then they've stood up for social justice.

Most of these "warriors" never leave the comfort of their homes to fight against what they believe is injustice. It is simply the idea of standing up for something that is enough. They then see themselves as righteous and forthright, and all others should see that in them too. The vast number of them would blanch away from what they would truly call a fight or even confrontation. It is quite easy to be brave sitting at a computer terminal with no one else around. There is no one there to confront you for your opinion.

Please remember to keep me apprised of the situation with the Christians. We need to track Ms. Bishop's reactions to this situation. We may need to consider bringing a male into the picture. This would complicate things nicely, giving her one more thing to worry about. Nothing is better than conflicted and confused feelings to stop a human in their tracks. I look forward to your next communication.

Your Infernal Mentor,

Shacklebolt
Master Tempter, I.T.B.

My bumbling protégé Pinegrub,

I am not happy with this situation. I have been very explicit with you. You were to keep the Christians AWAY from your charge. Ms. Bishop should have been easily handled in her confused and despairing state. That is the easiest time we have with these malformed mud monsters.

You admit to me you lost control of a being that was drawn forth from the mud! You tell me she has been actively speaking to the one group of people I've repeatedly instructed you to ensure she avoids! You tell me that one night you heard her actively praying for guidance from the Creator! And in all of that, YOU tell ME not to overreact!!!!

Who do you think you are, baby tempter, to tell one such as I not to overreact?!! I was dragging souls to hell long before you came to this existence!! I've forgotten more about corrupting the human soul than you will ever know! I've tasted the sweet nectar of their depression! I've listened to their wailings of despair that I helped to bring about!! I, who am highly regarded in the courts of our master!!! AND YOU TELL ME NOT TO OVERREACT!!!???

You sniveling insignificant whelp! I will show you an overreaction! You had better hope that this opportunity passes her by. All she has to do is reach out to her Creator in earnest. That is all! You have allowed her to hear the true Gospel message! You could have filled her ears with buzzing. You could have given her a headache. You could have drawn her attention somewhere else with a trick of the light and any one of a thousand other things.

Yet, you, who say that my reaction is overly strong, did nothing!!! You sat there like an impotent dandy your tail between your legs like a beaten dog. She freely listened to the story of the one who died to save her! You stood by and allowed the very thing that we sent you to her to prevent!!!

I warned you over and over to keep an eye on the Christians. I advised you to foster contempt for them in her mind. That was to ensure that if they called upon her, she would pay them no heed. There are reasons for everything I tell you. That is why I'm the teacher, and you are the student.

I have to say there was nothing of this rebellious streak in your file. I paid extreme attention to your file. It described a very willing and eager young demon that was inclined toward learning. One that was also appropriately servile to his superiors. You have been showing some alarming tendencies of late. I suggest you do whatever is needed to curb this attitude.

There is nothing for this now but to clean up your mess. Send a count of how many lower imps you have in the house. We must put the home in disarray to hide our efforts. I want you to enlist the aid of at least two of the lower imps. Have them harry the Christians day and night.

When they are sleeping or trying to sleep, have your underlings chanting at them. This will disrupt their sleep. In some humans, it keeps them from sleep entirely. The lack of sleep causes the monkeys to be less alert. This will aid in obscuring our actions.

During the daytime hours, have the imps cause as much mischief as they can. At this point in the game, we must pull out all the stops. This one is ours, and we mean to keep her. Tell the imps to cause fights. If they dig their claws into the skulls of the unsaved, it makes them vastly short-tempered.

I want you to ensure an attitude of complete unrest permeates the residence. The director of the home should be jumping at shadows. Everyone there should feel threatened at a very base level. During the day, use half of your remaining imps to crawl upon the unsaved, snarling into their ears.

According to your count, there are twelve females in the dwelling. Of the twelve, there are two practicing Christians. Those two will be under constant attack. Use the other half of your forces to cause gossip. See if you can cause an attitude of disgust toward Ms. Bishop. This will be easier than you might think.

I can assure you that there are at least two females in the home that think she is overreacting. They think her suffering is nothing compared to the unjust treatment they have received. To them, she is a weak and spineless girl, lacking the nerve to do what needs to be done.

They are the ones you will hear talking, alone in rooms in pairs. They will be saying things like, "I wouldn't have let that lady take my kids from me!" or possibly, "Lord, have mercy on the one who tries to get between my kids and me because I sure won't!"

The women talking like that are the ones you want to use to

divide the entire group. They have no compassion for someone that hasn't been through the wringer as they have. This is the type of behavior you see in hardened humans. They've seen the rougher side of their justice system because of their choices.

I want you to work on Ms. Bishop yourself. Convince her that the Christian's words were just pretty words. Whisper to her, the peace they seem to feel must be the power of suggestion. Call her attention to the strife they are dealing with now. That should be sufficient proof that this Christianity thing is just a phase.

You are to be as a leech on her. You will not leave her presence. Try to instill some animosity in her toward the Savior's children. Speak to her about how "If God is such a loving God, why is she slowly losing her children?" Focus on that pain and do everything you can to keep her mind on it.

Humans that are depressed and focused on their pain are much easier to manipulate. Keep the idea of how unfair the situation is. Persuade her that her children are beginning to forget her. Stay in constant contact with her physical form. You will be able to feel the shift in her emotions that way.

See if you can persuade one of the wandering tempters to take a look at the area. You need to know if the forces of the Father are nearby. The sudden shift in attention here has me bothered. I don't like being bothered. I hope this isn't the beginning of one of those stupid revivals.

It seems we need to deal with one of those about every generation. In times past, they were like forest fires. We were trying to keep the heavenly forces at bay while the followers of Christ were constantly praying. The revival times have sharply waned over the years. What was a yearly thing is now only happening once or twice in a human lifetime.

We have used the tool of the revival to draw more to ourselves. These are the false revivals. They contain the "feel good" Gospel, the "name it and claim it" Gospel, just to name a couple. It is quite an effective tool to draw those that want spirituality but don't want to commit to the true God. They still want their own spin on it.

While you see to my instructions, I will be speaking to Grand Tempter Jojun. The idea of the revival puts me ill at ease. I want to see if he knows of any movements in the heavenly forces in your area. We should be prepared rather than taken by surprise.

You need to understand that if their forces are on the move, it doesn't excuse your lack of diligence. There are signs that you should have noticed. An increase in prayer and a quiet peace settling over an area are two prominent telltale signs. If we can't undo the mess you've made, you will be punished. I will leave you with that thought.

Your Infernal Mentor,

Shacklebolt

Master Tempter, I.T.B.

My partially redeemed tempter Pinegrub,

I finally received your latest message. If you had made me wait much longer, I would have made a special visit to you. I am gratified, however, at your tidings. I was satisfied with the news that you had implemented all of my instructions. It would seem that you can take direction if you are properly motivated. I would hope that this degree of motivation isn't needed on a constant basis.

I must admit I was slightly surprised at your mention of the help you received from the envoy of Grand Tempter Jojun. I had known that he and I were respectful associates. I had not thought that he would leap into action so swiftly to aid our cause. We must remember this in the future. I'm sure the old demon will demand a favor or two from us in return.

That is one of the finer points of our work that you will have to learn. Nothing is free in our underworld. Everything that you get, you will earn. You may be granted a favor from some demon or tempter, but I promise you, you will pay for it. Take care in these types of dealings. In some situations, you end up paying much more than the favor was worth.

Your communication stated that the envoy brought five lesser imps and two tempters with him. That was a very generous gesture. You indicated, since you had the forces at your disposal, you doubled the numbers I recommended to you. That wasn't a bad decision, but you could have used one or two for recon duty. It is always a good idea to know what is going on around you.

The forces of good are constantly surrounding you. You have to keep in mind that we are fighting a battle that, ultimately, we can't win. The Creator has decreed we must lose in the end. How can we overcome One whose very word and will shape reality? Our aim is to do as much damage as we can. We attempt to deprive him of as many of his mud creatures as we can.

Since the subject is at hand, have you noticed any movement of the heavenly host? They have a way of moving without our knowledge. It is so frustrating. You work toward a goal for years. Then those goody-two-shoes idiots show up and ruin everything in a matter of days. Send me intelligence on any processes you have for gathering information on their doings.

The heavenly host especially pays attention to the prayers of these creatures. They call them "saints." Isn't that a laugh? They seem to be drawn to the ones who are in pain and crying out to the Creator. That is the main reason I keep telling you to interrupt the prayers of your charge. Keep them from prayer if you can. If you can't do that, then disrupt their prayers with idle thoughts or distractions. Prayer is one of their strongest weapons.

I was absolutely delighted to read of your progress with the two Christians in the house. It was very gratifying to read that the two house preachers got into a violent argument. You did exactly what you were supposed to do. You were able to cause them to forget their faith for the moment. They didn't think they were ambassadors for their Lord. They were completely centered on their own desires.
Try to remember this strategy. You will find it useful.

The fact that they were arguing about the attentions of a man is glorious. They are the Christians in the house. They are supposed to be the devout ones with the words of God on their hearts. In the eyes of the people of the world, they are supposed to be perfect. That argument did much to damage their witness to others.

Your letter stated that as their argument became heated, one called the other "a lying slut", and that is when the blows began to fall. I laughed with merriment at your description of them rolling on the floor, cursing as they fought. Nothing damages a burgeoning belief in Christ-like the hypocrisy and the exposure of blatant sin.

Keep in mind, their faith decries sin. They were fighting over a man, who by your description has no religious affiliation. This is wonderful. You have exposed their lustful sides. To the other females in the home, these two don't have their own stuff together. At this thought, how can they help anybody else?

Here is an excellent opportunity for you to damage their standing further. Prompt Anna to anonymously spread rumors of promiscuous behavior. Do it in such a way that it won't be traced back to her. We don't want to expose our hidden traitor yet. Keep her as our productive helper for as long as we can.

Have her watch the other girls at the meetings. They will undoubtedly socialize before or after with other females. See who is the most talkative with the females in the home. That one will be our gossip. That will be your first step.

Your second step should go something like this. Identify the woman you want to use. Have one of the imps follow her for a couple of days. You need to know what her habits are. If she has a job, find out where she works. Find out what she enjoys doing for a hobby. You need information on this person, so you can have Anna approach her.

When you have the information you need, wait for our devious Anna to pray. Go to her with our plot. You've told me of her ecstatic state when she hears your voice. I assure you; she will be overjoyed to help. Guide her to get to know our pawn.

Don't let Anna proceed to the gossip at first. Have her make friends with the stupid sheep. We want her to earn some trust before she starts feeding her misinformation. Ensure that Anna doesn't go to the meetings that this woman goes to. This will cause the rumors Anna gives her to be more believable.

Have our little turncoat suggest they meet for coffee in some pub across town. They will consider it their "friendship" spot. Make sure that the conversations stay on the interests both women have in common. Gradually guide the conversations from the pleasant and innocent to the more risqué.

It is during these conversations they will tend to open up to each other all the more. The silly sheep will believe that our Judas accepts her for who she is. It won't occur to her that she is to be a tool. She will carry on, blithely unaware of her part in this.

On their fourth meeting, not before, have Anna admit that she is a recovering alcoholic. This will strike a chord in the other woman. The sheep will then admit that she is herself a recovering alcoholic. They will then exchange stories of their journeys to recovery.

After this has happened, you can then compel Anna to begin the gossip campaign. Spread rumors of debauchery against both Christian women. Emphasize that they are given in the strictest confidence. It will be some time before either of the ladies find out what is being said about them. By then, their reputations will be so soiled that no one will listen to them about their faith.

This strategy will take longer than you like, but I promise it will be extremely effective. It will shake the foundations of trust for all of those involved. The Christians will be defamed in the eyes of those who thought to entertain the idea of following.

I know that I have practically fed you this strategy. It isn't my way of saying you are stupid. This is a tried-and-true strategy. Nothing muddies the waters like a bunch of lies. The trick is to have some good truth mixed in with the lies. There must be some good truth in the trail though. You can't lead someone around with only a pack of lies. That is too easily exposed.

In your next message, give me an update on the situation with the children. How has Ms. Bishop been handling her forced estrangement? Has she had any word from the social worker? Has her family made any attempt to contact her or to take the children? Have you been able to make any new inroads concerning her desire to drink? Details, I want details.

Your Infernal Mentor,

Shacklebolt

Master Tempter, I.T.B.

My hard-working young tempter Pinegrub,

I was very gratified at the news from your latest message. I was especially delighted to hear of the efficient use you've made of the imps in your employ. I will say I was rather leery of using the imps to influence the social worker in such a subtle way. I've never trusted those erratic creatures with anything of importance. They seem to me to be too unreliable.

In your writing, you stated that you used the imps to convince the social worker that she needed to do an in-depth investigation of Ms. Bishop. What chant did you have them repeat to her? I would imagine something like, "She is a bad mother." I don't see how that would spur an investigation. No matter how you did it, you did a good job. I would never have taken such a gamble in my younger years.

You said she went around the entire neighborhood asking for information on Ms. Bishop. I have a hard time believing that it was simple luck that led her to a disgruntled suitor. It isn't hard to believe that such a man would be happy to defame a woman who turned him down so many times.

I had thought that the immediate neighbor's testimony would have been sufficient. You seem to want to see how far you can push the situation. You want to be careful in that respect. If you push too far, it will reach the point of being ridiculous. At that point, a judge will see it more as a vendetta instead of a concern.

As things stand right now, you have completely blocked her efforts for visitation. It also appears that your efforts have left her almost no hope of regaining her privileges, let alone custody. Please send me more details on this. I would like to know what was said that yielded such stellar results.

I admit to a low chuckle and a wide grin when you told me of Ms. Bishop's reaction to the news. I have to say I envy you at moments like those. Was her despair sweet upon your tongue? Did you savor it or just gulp it down? These are the moments that are the most rewarding for you. Try not to squander them.

You can now truly say that you've achieved a milestone. You have succeeded in pushing a recovering alcoholic to drink. When I read that she'd used her weekend privileges to check into a hotel room and go on a binge, I laughed raucously.

Does the recovery home know what she has done? If they do,

what has been their reaction? You must be proactive in this. Post an imp on the house director. Have the imp repeat to her that there are no second chances for troublemakers. Ensure that she is reminded over and over of all the times that Tanya has been difficult. Try not to let empathy take root in her mind.

Those idiotic alcoholics preach a litany of no judgment for the fallen. Don't get me wrong, we are still able to cause a good bit of strife and condemnation among them. The problem is that the groundwork for forgiveness is already there. We have that working against us every time one of them has a relapse. It is a pain to deal with. It would've been so much easier if that portion of their program hadn't been instituted.

I don't think I need to tell you that you must keep this binge going for as long as you possibly can. The farther you push her out of the light and out of favor, the better. Her comrades will try to work with her for a time. However, they are creatures of time, and they won't hold on forever. If you can keep it up long enough, even her A.A. buddies will give up on her.

They do this out of a sense of self-preservation. If their associations don't give up their addiction, then they are left to their own devices. The sober or clean one doesn't want to be dragged down with them. They have an amusing saying concerning this. It goes, "If you hang around a barbershop long enough, you will end up getting a haircut."

I hope you realize that in her drunken and downtrodden state, she is much more susceptible to temptations of other sorts. She is in a hotel room alone, I take it. You could arrange for one of her male A.A. friends to come by to "checkup" on her. She is very weak and vulnerable now. A show of genuine concern from the opposite sex could cause her resistance to crumble. You could easily have her doing things she will heartily regret later.

Consider the shame that you will be able to add to her burdens. She will think herself a slut. She will remember all the times she has judged such women, and she will condemn herself for a hypocrite. Shame is wonderful fuel for self-condemnation. She will think of herself as a base whore. The irony is that she will be right.

These simple creatures don't consider that wishing you could commit a sin is the same as committing it in the Creator's eyes. The

Christ said in his "Sermon on the Mount," "You have heard that it was said, 'You shall not commit adultery.' But I tell you that anyone who looks at a woman lustfully has already committed adultery with her in his heart."

This is in their Bible, in the book of Matthew 5:27-28. The humans call it the NIV version. They truly don't realize the depth of their own iniquity. They can read things like this all their lives and never seem to be able to apply it to themselves. To most of them, the holy book is a collection of sayings for wisdom and some stories.

The churchgoers generally are just that. They go to church with the belief that going into a building once a week guarantees them a place in their heaven. A good number of them are so willful that they only go to church twice a year. They believe that going on the highest holy days is enough. They don't realize that by doing this, they are saying that the Creator should serve them, not the other way around.

You really should visit the local churches on Sundays for a while. You need to get a feel for what the churches are up to. You will see the heavenly host there. The good thing about seeing them in a church is they generally don't fight there. Generally, doesn't mean they don't. You still need to watch yourself.

What you see there will give you some insight into what they are doing and how they are operating. Unlike us, they work in an extremely strict command structure. None of them makes a move or acts without the permission of the throne of heaven. You can taunt them to their faces, and as long as you don't threaten their charges, the most they will do is look sternly at you.

I should make a point to note that you should never threaten their charge in their presence. That is the fastest way to see them draw a heavenly blade. I'm sure you already know that one swipe from their blade is enough to banish you to Sheol. It really isn't a fair fight. If you win the fight by stabbing your opponent, he will burst into a shower of sparks. He will then promptly reform at the throne of heaven.

When one of us is banished to Sheol, it is forever. We, unlike humans, can be released from the holding place by a powerful fallen angel. That does happen but not as much as you might hope. Remember what I told you about our forces dwindling. In the end times, our lord will be given the authority to throw open the gates and release our brethren. It is then that we will begin our all-out attack on the humans and their churches.

I advise you to keep your wits about you in the presence of the elect angels. Don't engage them in any way unless you are forced. Remember that you do have a claim over your charge while they remain unsaved. They can't simply take them from you. They also don't have the authority to simply run you away. Keep in mind though, that they can't lie. You can bluff. They can't.

If you do go to the local churches, take at least three imps with you. If you have one available, take one of the tempters. They are better for company and defense. The imps just run at the slightest rumbling of an angel.

Remember to let me know of your progress soon. You have reached a critical time with your charge. She is extremely depressed, and the humans have an annoying tendency to call out to the Father during those times. Keep her occupied and keep me informed.

Your Infernal Mentor,

Shacklebolt

Master Tempter, I.T.B.

My devilishly clever young tempter Pinegrub,

The news you send me keeps getting better and better. I see that you have ruined the reputation of Ms. Bishop in the home. I chortled with laughter when I read about the man you had delivered to her hotel room. How did you hit upon the idea to use the male the two Christian women were fighting over? I commend you for a stroke of genius.

You have, in one stroke, isolated a downtrodden woman and discredited the followers of Christ by their reaction to her. The other women in the home see these ladies' anger toward Ms. Bishop. They preach forgiveness and love until a man comes along. Don't think for an instant that it escapes the notice of others.

One thing you can be sure of. When a person expresses their devotion to the Creator and his Christ, everyone watches them. I believe it is a compulsion. They want to see that individual fall into sin. Then they can point and say, 'See? That Christianity thing doesn't work. They are still the same old person they were before.'

I advise you to put at least one imp on the Christians for the time being. Have the imps repeat to the ladies that their man has been stolen by a slut. Tell them to say that Tanya seduced the poor man in a drunken state. They will believe that he was led away by seduction and will regard her as a slut even more.

I noticed that you didn't send me any information concerning the house director. Has your campaign on that front been successful? Is it stalled? I hope you don't tell me that the director is in a forgiving frame of mind. That would be most unfortunate. In your next message, apprise me of this situation.

Has Ms. Bishop returned to the rooms of A.A.? Has she taken the ignoble walk to receive her twenty-four-hour chip again? That seems to be a huge point of contention for humans. They absolutely hate to have to admit to failing at the same thing over and over. It is one of the reasons that attendance at the meetings drop off sharply after some time in the program.

What of the man that was her partner in the hotel room? Has your charge had any contact with him since her return to the home? Please tell me that they are still in contact by secret text messages. Nothing causes trouble like a controversial secret relationship. That would make this so much more delicious.

What can you tell me of Ms. Bishop's sponsor? Have they had a parting of the ways? Does she even have a sponsor anymore? If you need, let me know, and I will see about steering a couple of worldly old biddies your way. I think we might have a yoga/Wiccan practitioner we can put into play.

Please tell me that you are arranging for the social worker to hear of this latest binge. I would say that our crafty helper (Anna) would be a good anonymous informer for that tidbit. She doesn't need to identify herself. Just ensure that she calls the social worker's office and leaves a message. Ensure that she urges a trip to the recovery home for corroboration.

That will be another nail in the coffin of visitation. I do so love it when we have one of these creatures so turned around. Ms. Bishop is sure to be so lost now that she doesn't know which way is up. You have the advantage at the moment. Keep increasing the pressure. She believes she's lost all hope for her children. Now take away her friendly surroundings.

If her playmate at the hotel is still in play, see if you can prompt him to pay a visit to the home. You indicate that he is stupidly unaware of the other ladies' interest in him. His presence in the home will cause a goodly amount of strife. If you play your cards right, you could be well on your way to turning this woman into a street tramp.

How is Anna's situation in the house? I do hope she hasn't given herself away. It is still too early in this game to lose a valuable player due to stupidity. She needs to come across as the most forgiving, the most understanding. It will come as such a shock to the others when her true nature is revealed.

A way to enhance the shock is to have Anna fake a Christian conversion. If she pretends heartily to be a Christian while taking direction from your promptings, we can have the home discredited or even shut down. Imagine the damage we can do to the Christian community in the area with one hidden wolf in sheep's clothing.

I am not saying that this is the direction you should choose. You have a wide range of options now. I am just offering ideas at the moment. You may see more from your point of view. Sometimes, when you are in the field alone, you are forced to make snap decisions from your gut. You are showing that you are capable. You should have the confidence that you see what needs to be done.

Let me urge you, though, to take my advice concerning Anna and the tipoff to social services. The message she leaves should be with a secretary. You don't want her voice to be recorded. That could come back to bite you. A nice anonymous message will do what you need right now. The rest you have some time to think about.

You neglected to mention what you learned of the local churches. For some reason, our intelligence in that region is sorely lacking. We can't see in that area because of the prayer cover. We think that there is a core of individuals there sincerely keeping and spreading their faith.

They are the worst kind of adversary. They are happy all the time, no matter the circumstance. They genuinely have faith in the Lord who bought them. They aren't like the ones that fall after a small trial. They tend to get stronger the longer they hold on. They are like a weed in our infernal garden.

When you go to look at the local churches, LIKE I KNOW YOU WILL, there are some things you need to pay attention to. The prayer cover that I mentioned above is one of them. It will appear to your eyes to be a misty, bright, white cloud. Stay away from it at all costs. You do not want to get caught in the middle of a prayer stream. It will take you weeks or possibly months to heal from the burns.

You also need to listen closely as you near the premises of a church. If you hear any music that might be praise, be on your highest guard. Where there is praise, the host of heaven is never far away. They are drawn to it like maggots to filth.

Here is a tactic that I've found to be effective. Allow yourself to sink into the ground. You are an extra-dimensional being. You can alter your density and your perceptions so that you can perceive the world around you. I've found that angels spend a great deal of time in the company of humans. Because of this, sometimes they forget to look around in different ways.

What I just told you isn't an invisibility cloak. If they want to look around for an intruder, they will. Your job is to be so stealthy that they have no reason to suspect your presence. If they do become aware of you, your best course of action is to run. Run like your existence depends on it because much of the time it does.

It is a good idea to take another tempter with you when you are going into a possible enemy stronghold. If the two of you are discovered, you will be able to split up. That will gain you a moment of indecision on the part of your enemies. A moment is all you need to get away safely.

If you can't find another tempter to go with you, take an imp. They are at least good fodder to draw angelic attention. Use scare tactics to threaten the tiny beast into silence before you go. If you are discovered, promptly grab the annoying little pest and throw him at the angels as you run for your life. Survival of the fittest and all that, you know.

Remember to send me the information that I've asked for above. I also WANT a recon of the local churches. I mean, I REALLY want a recon of the local churches. We need more information on the enemy's activities. I leave the rest in your obviously capable hands. Keep me informed and remember. Details, I need details.

Your Infernal Mentor,

Shacklebolt
Master Tempter, I.T.B.

My stellar pupil, Pinegrub,

I am beside myself with joy at reading your message. You have outdone yourself, young one. Your report indicates that you worked in concert with two other tempters. That is an accomplishment in and of itself. As you already know, our kind isn't cooperative at all. We generally only understand domination and punishment.

You stated that Ms. Bishop had to be restrained in the courtroom when she went into hysterics. I wish I could have been there when she was informed that her parental rights were terminated. It sounds like the moment was positively scrumptious.

I see that the judge was highly insulted by the profane names she called him. Not only that, but she assaulted her lawyer, calling him a worthless piece of crap. Now the poor dear has been found in contempt of court. Is she still in jail as you read this, or has she been released?

Other than her stint in jail, what other punishment does she face? Is she going to pay a large fine? Is she on probation? Is she facing a trial by a jury of her peers? I specifically remember telling you that I needed details when you send me a report. We are going to have to work on this issue.

In your next report, I would like a briefing on your charge's state of mind. Let me know what consequences she is facing. Have her housemates gathered around her or turned from her? Has she found another sponsor? If so, what is their relationship?

Do you know if she will be allowed back in the house? Is she to be evicted or placed on some sort of house probation? Do you know if she has any sort of plan if she has no house to go back to?

I know you still have the taste of victory in your mouth, but this is only the beginning. You are on your way to winning the war, but you've only won skirmishes so far. You have this woman on the run; this is true. The issue at hand is that you haven't defeated her utterly. She will be utterly defeated when the last breath leaves her body, and she is ushered into the realm of torments.

You must stay on your guard. The Creator has a terrible habit of forgiving these creatures at their last breath. You have to keep this woman from turning to the Father. If you allow her a moment's peace, she will begin to seek some peace of mind. At this point in time, right now, you have her reeling. You must make your best effort to keep her that way.

Let us assume for the moment that she will be allowed back into the house. Their business is to help these vagabonds recover from their addictions. The owner of the home generally gets into this business out of personal interest. Recovery homes are usually owned by a single or group of recovering alcoholics or addicts.

She will probably be allowed back into the home on a restricted basis. She will only be allowed to go to work and recovery meetings. Other than that, she will be assigned chores and possibly training by writing pages of a recovery manual. The training would be much more effective if it were voluntary, but this will be punishment as much as training.

When she gets back into the home, she will be contrite at first. They are all like that. When she settles into a comfortable routine, her attitude will undergo a shift. She will go back to her former behavior. They do this because what is familiar is comfortable. She will even be easily angered if her motives are questioned soon after her infraction.

What I have mentioned so far is to be expected. What you have to do now is form a plan that takes these situations and actions into account. You must turn her contrition to your advantage. You have to use her expected impatience with those around her. She will be proceeding under the thought, "Don't they see I'm trying?" Those around her will only see temporary compliance.

I see that you've found a few things about the young man she was with. So, he was only playing a part? I love that. He was pretending to be a concerned and confused friend. I wish I could have been there to see the reaction on Ms. Bishop's face. Your communication stated that he didn't want anything to do with Ms. Bishop now that he has "hit that." That is so amusing.

Are his attitude and true colors common knowledge, or has Ms. Bishop kept this to herself? If it is common knowledge, his usefulness to us is all but spent. If it isn't, then he will be a useful pawn in the rumor mill. Don't forget you have two Christian women in the home. They seem willing enough to forget their faith for this young man.

We could possibly ruin some evangelistic opportunities here. Nothing stops Christian witness faster than lies or promiscuity. How can you claim to be a child of God when you blatantly flaunt his commandments? Find out what you can about this angle. I would be exceedingly interested in seeing what we can do to the two supposedly devout followers of the Creator.

I didn't see anything in your report concerning our anonymous traitor. Is Anna still playing the double agent, or have you given her rest for the time being? Don't waste a highly valuable asset. Keep her in play for as long as you can shield her actions.

Have you had Anna text Ms. Bishop to see how she is doing? We must keep up the façade of friendship. Ensure that Anna expresses worry for her 'friend'. That is a point of contact that we have worked too hard to preserve to just throw away.

Don't forget herd mentality as a venue of attack. Since your randy young buck has had his way with Ms. Bishop, ensure that he spreads the word. His fellows in the program will begin to pay her much more attention. Her reputation as a slut will grow just from the telling. She will probably form at least one close relationship from it due to her isolation alone.

In all these preparations and opportunities, don't forget the technological angle. Your charge's cell phone is one of your most useful tools. You need to draw her attention back into it. She needs friends who understand her now. Speak to the other tempters in the area. See if any of them know of an online support group for mothers who have lost their rights.

You want to get her dependent on her phone. The more you keep her on her phone chatting, texting, and posting things to her Facebook account, the more you distance her from the real world. Speak to the other tempters in the meetings. See if you can get a steady stream of texting to and from Ms. Bishop to her "friends."

At the point that she has a goodly number of conversations going on her phone, prompt the director of the house. Have the imps repeat to her that Tanya isn't involved enough in her program. Remind her that every time she sees Ms. Bishop, she is on her phone. She can use this as grounds to confiscate the phone. After all, she will be doing it for her own good.

Your charge will react in one of two ways. Here is possibility number one. She will be outraged and refuse to give up her little technological crutch. If this is the case, the director will have grounds to contact the owner of the home. In the event of total non-compliance Ms. Bishop can be ejected from the home.

Possibility number two will go something like this. After some grumbling, Ms. Bishop will placidly hand over her phone. She will strongly feel that it is unjust but won't have the authority to refuse. This will drive her batty.

She will wonder if the house director is going through her phone without her permission. She will feel as though her privacy has been invaded. She will wonder what she is missing. She will feel disconnected from the things where she is drawing solace. This will cause her attitude to take a significant downturn.

Consider the advice I've provided to you. Implement what you can. Let me know how much you've been able to make Ms. Bishop dependent on her phone. Let me know about her employment status. Has her stint in jail lost her job? What is her reputation with the employment agencies? That is something we could possibly attack. Remember that we are trying to remove hope from this woman.

Also, provide me with an overview of the people she interacts with at the meetings. That is going to be her only outlet for a time. We need to sour the milk there as well. You are doing a good job knocking the underpinning out of her life. By the time she realizes it, she will feel completely hopeless. Keep me posted.

Your Infernal Mentor,

Shacklebolt

Master Tempter, I.T.B.

My tireless tempter, Pinegrub,

My, my, my, haven't you been busy young one. This has been the longest and most detailed report I've received. By your report, you have been receiving advice and aid from your fellow tempters. The advice that you have received seems to indicate the touch of Grand Tempter Jojun. I find that very curious. It is welcome news that you send me concerning your charge, but I begin to wonder at motives.

Your helpers aren't aiding you out of the goodness of their hearts. Remember who you are dealing with. They have no goodness in their hearts. They are demons and sometimes a fallen angel. They have goals of power inside our structure. Do you think they are just friendly and helpful?

Make no mistake about the help you are receiving. They want something from you, or they want something from someone near you. They might possibly be seeking the downfall of someone near you. You are too new to your occupation to have made many enemies in this venue. Consider well your actions in the near future.

That is enough of the dire warnings. Now on to business. Your list of accomplishments is growing. I see that you have caused your charge to go on yet another binge. She is blaming the court case and her treatment by her peers for her downfall. If you hadn't noticed it already, that is a typical human response.

They seldom, if ever, take responsibility for their immoral actions. It is always someone else's fault. Several decades ago, an old adage became popular in western culture. "The devil made me do it" was a very well-used saying. We must admit, they get it honestly. When confronted with disobedience in the garden, Adam blamed Eve, who in turn blamed the serpent.

None of them want to face their iniquity. It isn't a pretty picture. A human has a hard time facing the things they have done that violate their personal code of morals. Notice that I didn't say God's moral code. Most of them don't recognize His moral code as theirs. Even so, when they are reminded of a personal failure, they rationalize it and move on to something else quickly.

The damage that this latest binge has caused will be irreparable in the mind of Ms. Bishop. I must admit to being surprised at the extreme she went to this time. You realize that this latest act was an act of rebellion? She isn't getting anything she wants, so she is acting out. You must further deny her desires. If you frustrate her now, you can rob her of all hope.

It must have taken a concerted effort on the parts of yourself and the other tempters helping you. From your reports, I never thought of Tanya Bishop as a woman interested in group sex. Did you use multiple tempters on the participants to ensure coercion? I would not have thought a junior tempter could have managed to entice a woman like Ms. Bishop into group sex with four men at the same time. I believe the humans call the act a gang bang.

I can just imagine the flavor of the emotions you and your cronies enjoyed. You drew satisfaction from the success of the temptation. Now you can draw more of the same from reminding her of her actions. It is as I have told you. You get them coming and going. You tempt them into sin and, then you, the tempter, enjoy condemning them for the selfsame sin.

Her reputation in the house and in the local A.A. chapter is ruined. The only interest the men will have for her is sexual. The only response she will receive from the females will be hostile. They will see her as a threat to any relationship they may have. The only females that will consider a friendship with her will be the ones who have "been there, done that."

She will see herself now as nothing more than a base slut. In her own mind, she could rationalize the tryst with the young man. This is something she can't get away from. Every good little girl knows that more than one partner at a time is simply wrong.

Let us move on to more material issues. The house director has sufficient reason now to eject her from the home. She can cite disharmony in the house caused by Tanya's actions. That will force Ms. Bishop to examine her dwindling options. At this time, her choices should be a precious few.

Does she have any friends or friendly acquaintances left? Is there anyone that she hasn't offended to the point of turning away from her? We can use her latest actions, her loss of her place in the home, along with the loss of her children, to push her depression to the extreme.

I believe now would be a good time for Anna to reveal herself to Ms. Bishop. She shouldn't do it in front of anyone. Make it a private affair. That way, Anna can claim that your charge is spreading lies in addition to her horrendous behavior. Then our trusting subject will see that her best friend has been her betrayer. That reminds me a bit of what happened when our dark master prompted Judas to betray the Son of man.

I can tell you from experience. You will genuinely enjoy the fruit of betrayal when Anna reveals herself. Prompt her to play the innocent. When she reveals herself, she should come across as hurt and let down by someone she looked up to. What else could she do but tell the house director of Tanya's behavior?

Prompt Anna to come across as worried about her friend. The whole time she should radiate arrogance. This will cause your charge to feel self-loathing and anger at Anna at the same time. Let it slip out that Anna feels disappointed and let down by Ms. Bishop.

When they start to argue, and trust me, they will, prompt our cunning traitor. Get her to say something along the lines of, "I should have known better than to be friends with such a man-hungry slut!" Along with that, she should reveal that all the men in their A.A. group are looking for some easy action.

If it comes to blows, and it very well may, prompt Anna to fear and flight. If she flees while she is being beaten, there is a good chance the other women of the house will come to her rescue. This will absolutely seal Ms. Bishop's ejection from the home immediately.

I want you to understand completely what we are trying to accomplish. We are stealing all of Ms. Bishop's hope. She has no hope of regaining her children. She has thrown away her self-respect and self-esteem. It is likely that she is lower than she has ever been. This is the time that we need to capitalize on.

When she is thrown from the house, keep at least three imps on her. Don't give her a single moment of peace. Have them chant at her constantly. Tell her how worthless she is as a woman. Tell her she was a terrible mother, and her children are far better off without her.

Continually bemoan the fact that all her friends have deserted and turned on her. She has nowhere to go where people want her around. She is unwelcomed in the rooms of recovery. Her own family doesn't even want her.

For this strategy to work, you must keep her dwelling on her situation. Don't give her a moment to seek spiritual aid. If she wants to curse God for her situation, that is fine. At all costs, however, you are not to allow her to reach out to the Father. It is when they are at their lowest that he answers. Words can't explain how frustrating it is when that happens.

This is the point where we make it or break it. This set of circumstances will drive her further from the light than she has ever been, or it will drive her straight into the arms of the Savior. She can't turn to the light if we keep her eyes and mind in the dark. Depression is the best weapon we have in this instance.

Send me a detailed report of everything that happens over the next forty-eight hours. Keep in mind the things I've noted above. Do everything you can to keep the elect angels away from her. She is ours. I have a feeling that the next message I get from you will be extremely good news or extremely bad. Keep in mind this is your first success, or it is your first failure.

Your Infernal Mentor,

Shacklebolt

Master Tempter, I.T.B.

My Victorious tempter, Pinegrub,

Words can't express the pride I feel in you. You came to me an inexperienced messenger demon. Now you are coming along nicely as a tempter. I have to say you have picked up your trade swiftly, little one. Not many fresh tempters drive their first charge to suicide, but you managed it.

I am not so dense that I don't realize you had help. I have warned you of the consequences of accepting help. You are, as they say, the man in the field. Decisions while in action are yours to make. Try to exercise some caution while you make them. Those are demons that you are dealing with. Sooner or later, they are going to want their pound of flesh in payment.

Enough of warnings; this is a time of celebration. I was pleased to see that you are continuing to provide me with the details for which I have been berating you. I suspect you may have accepted some pointers in that area as well. Your communications have vastly improved in that department.

I especially enjoyed the portion of your message that talked about the argument. You stated that she hadn't been in the A.A. meeting for five minutes before the remarks started to fly. That is typically how humans get a fight started. They will make small remarks about each other, attempting to appear as they are talking to someone else.

For instance, if Mary is mad at Jill for wearing her blouse without permission, the dialog would go something like this.

> **Mary speaking to someone else in the room**, "I would never take something from someone else without permission."
> **Jill taking up the gauntlet**, "I didn't take it. I borrowed it."
> **Mary turned to Jill**, "What do you call it when you take someone's possessions without their permission? I was brought up to believe that is the definition of stealing."
> **Jill beginning to show ire**, "Are you calling me a thief?!"
> **Mary**, "Did you take something without permission?"

From there, it would devolve to name-calling and threats until one or the other worked up the courage to get physical.

Your report said that Ms. Bishop and her opponent were physically restrained by four men in the room. Don't you find it delicious that her opponent was one of the so-called devout Christians? The fact that this Christian woman didn't have any infernal prompting from any tempter or imp shows how well you've done your job.

I know the self-righteous Christian doesn't see it, but her behavior damaged her witness for Christianity. There isn't a single person that was in that room who will go to her for spiritual advice. She branded herself a Christian hypocrite when she picked the fight. That is one of the small bonuses you get to pick up on the way to your goal.

Now we get on with the meat of the message. I was deliriously happy to read that you have succeeded in causing Ms. Bishop to commit suicide. I will say that the method she chose was very unoriginal. I mean, who cuts their wrists in these times? Most of our suicide victims are afraid of pain. It is much easier to give yourself an overdose on your drug of choice. Then there is the tried-and-true sleeping pill method. The method of choice doesn't matter. What matters is the result, and you, my good (or should I say bad) demon, have gotten those.

I see by your report that you weren't the only tempter in the room when she did the deed. I don't see how you allowed this. You were the one who put in the work. You are the one who is responsible for your failure or your victory. Considering this, why would you share your victory with someone who was only on the sidelines? Once again, this was your choice. I may be getting old. I simply don't understand your generation of demonkind.

As I understand from your report, Tanya left the meeting in a humiliated rage. She was nursing the beginnings of a bruise on her face from the altercation. You also said that she had blood under her nails after raking them across the face of that fine Christian woman. Did you do anything to collect the blood? The life is in the blood. I can put you in touch with a young sorceress who could use it to our advantage.

Ms. Bishop went from the meeting straight to the liquor store. Isn't it funny how the A.A. clubhouse is usually near a liquor store? You stated that the store associate seemed genuinely concerned about her. You need to understand that most men who work in a liquor store are there to make money. If he was concerned about her, it was probably sexual in nature. He could have been worried about the attention this battered woman might bring to his establishment.

She went from there to the motel that she had been in the weekend before. You stated that the manager of the motel was giving her a leer as he gave her the key to her room. I realize that for you, the goal was in sight. However, you could have used the opportunity of the manager to pour even more shame on this woman. They are our enemy. We leave them no dignity if we can accomplish it.

You say she went into the room and proceeded to get staggeringly drunk. In the process of drinking, she took out the pictures of her children and laid them out across the nightstand. You said the entire time she was doing this, you were berating her.

You told her what a rotten mother she was. You dug your claws into her skull while you screamed that she was a worthless tramp. You had imps fly through her body while you reminded her that she would never have her children. You reminded her that everyone she thought was her friend had turned on her.

You alluded to the conversation between our crafty Judas and her. You never gave me any real details about it. You stated that Anna admitted that she had gone to the house director because she was worried about Tanya. You never said anything of what came of the conversation. I assume that Ms. Bishop left the house feeling extremely betrayed.

You say she drank and cried over her children. You enjoyed her depression, and you called it a sense of gloom. You extolled the joy you felt at her despair. You were able to prompt her to write a note saying that she had nothing left to live for. Her children were gone. Her family had deserted her, and her friends had abandoned her. Her life was in a shamble of her own making. She was so deeply sorry for the pain she'd caused and resolved to end it all. She rummaged through her purse and found the penknife her father had given her years ago.

You said that when she got up to go to the bathroom, the whole game was almost blown. Her phone rang, and the number that came up was her former sponsor. Before she saw the number, you were able to cause her to stumble and knocked the phone from her hand. You were able to guide the cell phone into the toilet, where it promptly shorted out. I would have to say that was quick thinking on your part.

She removed her clothing while the tub filled with hot water. Your message stated that she got into the tub and used the penknife in a very businesslike manner. She cut herself along the tops of her forearms from wrist to elbow. I would have to say she was a determined woman at that point. Most people flinch at the beginning of such pain. To have done both arms, in the same manner, is almost remarkable.

Your description of how she died in a tub of blood with tears streaming down her face was almost poetic. I didn't know you had that degree of melancholy in you. Did you hide when the death angel approached? Did you see her eyes open on the real reality for the first time? Did she see you? Did you see a flash of recognition of just who you are and what you'd done to her? Did you enjoy her confused wailing as she was dragged away to her doom?

I have to say that I find some inconsistencies in your messages. It is almost as though you are writing them in collaboration. Here are some questions. Are you in collaboration, and what is your aim? I have been your teacher and your mentor. I have tried to guide you on the wisest path of your mission. What is it that you are trying to affect?

I give you full credit for achieving your goal. You have helped our side to yet another victory. Hers is one soul the Father will never cradle again. You have done your job well. I believe we may have to have a face-to-face meeting soon.

In the meantime, congratulations on a job well done. I will begin the search for your next charge. I will be in touch as soon as one is found for you.

Your Infernal Mentor,

Shacklebolt

Master Tempter, I.T.B.

My twisted, inexperienced, traitorous tempter, Pinegrub,

It appears that some of my questions have been answered without your participation. I was just released from a tribunal where I was the accused. Imagine my sense of confusion as I relaxed on the shoulder of my host, and a demon lord snatched me in his claws and screamed the word "Traitor" in my face with no small amount of vitriol.

I must admit to a great swell of fear in the beginning. I wasn't informed of the offense to which I was accused. I was bound hand and foot and dragged into a thriving church. The church was holding a prayer meeting. The so-called saints were all bowed or kneeling in prayer. There were a few who were on their face before their Lord.

The Holy Spirit was present in that place in force. He was moving from saint to saint, comforting and whispering. The place was dripping with love and adoration for the Father. Praise and prayer were wafting through the air like perfume, and it burned me.

I lay in the closet of that church for hours burning and screaming. The blisters that were raised from sincere, faithful praise would burst and bleed, only to be replaced with more. At one point, my left eye boiled away, and my ears melted. All I could do was scream. There was no coherence left in me.

When the prayer meeting was over, I thought I might be given some respite. I had thought that someone would come and question me. I thought this was a misunderstanding that could be cleared up soon. I was wrong.

The demon lord who captured me gathered me up in a net. He and two of his minions carried my abused and burned body to yet another church. It would seem, prayer meetings go on at all hours. I was beaten and kicked until my bones were shattered. This made it much easier for them to stuff me into a small bag.

They placed the bag under the altar of the church. There were at least ten saints on their faces before the altar. All of them were offering earnest prayers and praises to the God of the universe. Each time they cried out to Jesus felt like an electrified chainsaw ripping through my brain.

Have you ever been bound so tightly that it hurt to take a breath? I was. I couldn't draw in a breath to scream, but scream was all my broken body wanted to do. I couldn't move. I couldn't blink because my remaining eye was swelled shut. They prayed, and it felt like being wrapped in a blanket of fire while red hot hooks pulled at my insides.

I was half delirious from the pain, but I heard the group planning another prayer meeting. They planned it for the following night. I prayed to the infernal prince to end my suffering, but that wasn't to be. When the prayer meeting ended, the demon lord approached the altar and yelled from a distance. "Enjoy tomorrow's prayer meeting, traitor!"

The next night was even worse. The group had told their friends how the power of God was moving in the church. From what I could hear, there were at least twenty-five worshippers there. They prayed and sang for what seemed like an eternity. I lay there, alternately trying to scream and gritting my teeth until they cracked.

The meeting came to a crescendo when a deaf woman was brought into the church. The entire congregation prayed over her and for her. The Holy Spirit answered the prayers of his saints. The wretched female received her hearing for the first time in her life. At that point, I felt like I was lying in a river of lava.

Screaming did no good. Gritting my teeth did no good. Praying to our infernal master did no good. When you are suspected of wrongdoing or collaboration, mercy is not an option. It seems our ilk deal in punishment long before getting to the question of guilt or innocence. It may have been easier to bear if I had but known the reasons for my punishment.

At the end of the third night's meeting, I was a puddle of pain and searing burns. We heal almost instantly, given that we are spirit beings. None of the wounds inflicted by the prayer or praise had begun healing. My bones couldn't heal because of my position in the bag. You would think a bag would be easy to escape. That is not so. When you have no leverage, you can apply no real strength.

Several hours after the meeting was over, I was released from the bag. The demon lord came in with his minions. They opened the bag, and I was unceremoniously poured to the foot of the still boiling hot altar. I lay there in a broken puddle, trying in vain to straighten my limbs.

The demon lord screamed that I was accused of treason and would be questioned by the prince of the domain. His minions lifted me up by my arms, dislocating both in the process. They bound my dislocated arms behind my back and blindfolded me. I didn't see much reason for the blindfold. My missing eye hadn't grown back, and the other was still swollen shut.

I was dropped to the floor, where the demon lord kicked me repeatedly. He screamed that I was a disgusting traitor the whole time he abused me. I believe he was able to shatter at least four of my ribs before he grew tired of the game.

His last kick was a glancing blow to my head. It actually knocked away the scab holding my eye shut. As I lay there on my side, rasping and whimpering, I could see that he was enjoying himself. The look of demented glee was in his eyes as he sank his fangs into my lower leg.

They finally tired of the punishment when I was rendered too insensible to scream. If I had known the screaming was what kept it going, I would have found a way to stop sooner. A few more bites and a few raking talons down my back, and they gave up.

The larger minion slung me across his back, and they took flight. We flew for some indeterminable amount of time before we passed through the walls of an old burned-out church. It was a large building. It must have been rather stately in its time. The sanctuary had been converted into a crumbling throne room.

I was dumped at the foot of the desecrated altar. A throne of sorts had been put in place. The largest demon lord I've ever seen sat upon the throne. He looked down at me with disdain and spoke to me in my mind. He offered me a choice.

I could willingly let him have my thoughts for examination. That way, he would know without doubt if I was a traitor as he'd been told. My other option was to resist him. He would then force his way into my mind as violently as possible. The last option would leave me a drooling idiot for eons to come. We heal quickly, but wounds of the mind are extremely slow to heal.

I, of course, chose the first option. I was basely violated. I tried not to resist, but I knew he could sense my aversion. He savored my pain and my humiliation. He was not gentle with me by any means. He found my humiliation to be amusing. He was so strong. I could not have stopped him if I had tried.

He sifted through every thought I've ever had. Cackling with laughter, he tore away my sense of self-worth. It was explained to me that I was merely a tool in the hands of an uncaring master. I was nothing special or even average. I was one of the lowly.

Finally, he threw me away, stating that this was just a false alarm. It seemed that my junior tempter had exaggerated my words and behavior to a Grand Tempter named Jojun. Jojun had, of course, reported the breach of our laws as a duty. The duty seemed to bring him no small amount of glee.

I was told to straighten out my affairs upon pain of further punishment. Matters of this low priority should not be brought before the prince. I was not allowed to speak in my defense. I was told that nothing in my authority has changed and that I was responsible for this incident.

I was allowed to crawl away without further molestation. I lay in an unused sewer pipe for the next few days while my wounds healed. The entire time I lay there, racked with pain, I thought of you. I had undergone all this agony and suffering because of you. It would be a fair assumption on your part to assume that I am not happy with you.

Now that I am back in my home, I need to get about the business of acquiring you a new charge. I also need to think of a suitable way to instruct you on the proper behavior of a junior tempter toward his master tempter. Don't worry. I will be very thorough. I intend to teach you the meaning of vengeance.

Your Furious Infernal Mentor,

Shacklebolt
Master Tempter, I.T.B.

My sniveling, cowardly junior tempter, Pinegrub,

I received your last message and paid it no more than a passing glance. I am not interested in your bumbling attempts at apology. Nor do I care to hear about how you were led into this by another. If you remember, I gave you ample warnings along the way down your traitorous walk. Now you will begin to pay the price.

Notice that this message started out the same way all my other messages began. The word "My" is not a figure of speech. You are MINE! You obviously need to be taught what that means. I take pleasure in informing you that I've been turning over in my mind the best way to educate you on that fact.

I have spoken to your partner in crime. Grand Tempter Jojun denies any plotting on his part. He, of course, explained that your words alarmed him, and he was merely doing his duty. He expressed sorrow for the pain that was mistakenly inflicted upon me.

He was lying to me in the same way he was lying to you. I was intelligent enough to recognize it, however. I suspected that something was afoot but couldn't pin down what my newest junior tempter was up to. I didn't dream that you would have turned on me so early in your instruction.

I will remind you that you were given the choice to join the legion of the tempters. You accepted that offer. Along with the benefits of this post, you also accepted the rules and discipline. Disobeying an order from your master tempter is a punishable offense. I'm sure you saw the examples of the punishment reserved for traitors.

As far as this subject is concerned, I will remind you that you MUST obey my every order. A shrewd master would use his authority to have his junior tempter punish himself in the line of his duties. While the fear and the apprehension build inside you, I will give you the information on your next charge.

Jamal Williams is your next charge. He is a 27-year-old African American male. He is the offspring of a so-called "Baptist" preacher. His mother is a very strong-willed woman who doesn't respect her husband's spiritual leadership. He grew up listening to his parents constantly fight over familial leadership and money.

He wasn't led into Christianity as a child so much as herded with a whip and a great deal of disapproval. Jamal didn't get into a lot of trouble, but a few of his friends did. He was berated a great deal by his father on his choice of friends. He tried on more than one occasion to explain to his father that he wasn't making choices for his friends.

The young man has a keen mind. The question "Why?" is ever on his mind. This will not be a man to put his faith in anything blindly. Two days after his high school graduation, he saw his father leaving the home of a well-known prostitute. The young man never bothered to confront his father about it. On his eighteenth birthday, he enlisted in the army and walked away from his parent's faith.

During his time in the military, he did quite a bit of growing. After a bit more than a year away from home, he started opening the letters from his mother. It took a few months for him to put the pieces together. The young man figured out that he was mistaken about his father. The family took a slow path to restoration.

Jamal's mind was radically changed when he found out the truth about the local prostitute. His parents were counseling the woman at her request. She had just found out that one of her regulars had tested positive for HIV. She had since found out that she hadn't contracted the disease. That scare was the wake-up call she needed.

On the occasion that Jamal had seen his father leaving the home, he was only going to their car for some study material. His mother was in the house. If the young man had waited a few minutes or confronted his father, he would have found the truth at that time.

When all of this was brought to light for him, things changed. He realized how wrong he was about his parents. He had harbored feelings of hatred for his father. He thought his father a religious hypocrite. He had regarded his mother as a bossy, intolerant woman. After all, if she were a submissive wife, then they wouldn't have argued so much.

He realized his father wasn't a lying cheater. His mother, while trying to be a properly respectful wife, still had ideas of her own. They would have loud debates but never degraded to cursing or blatantly disrespectful remarks. Neither of his parents was perfect, but they were serious about their faith and their marriage.

The process of the young man coming to a "saving" faith was somewhat convoluted. He is an intelligent young man, and he'd grown up around the faith. Even though he hadn't occupied the faith, he had the eyes to see what was obviously true. All that was needed was the stripping away of his pride. The army did that for him.

Jamal had lived a sheltered life up to the point he'd joined the army. He made several acquaintances in Basic Training that were more than willing to lead him into the wilder side of life. He did sample a few of the darker temptations to which young Christians fall prey. We almost had him a couple of times.

After his basic and advanced training, he was assigned to his first permanent duty station. He ran into a few of his "friends" from training. They tended to hang around together after duty hours. Something about hardship forms a bond between humans.

He tried the weekend drinking that so many of his barracks mates were doing. At first, it was a good time. Then the morning hangovers let him know he had no real tolerance for it. Unlike his friends, his second hangover taught him that if it made him that sick, it wasn't good for him.

During one of his few binges, he did what had caused him to curse his father. One of his acquaintances led him to a house of ill repute. Jamal had a sense of what the place was but wasn't exactly sure. The girl who approached him was incredibly attractive. He wasn't so drunk that he couldn't have said no.

Between his friends pressuring him to "Go ahead and do it" and the girls enticing wheedling, he gave in. He couldn't say no in front of his friends. They would have thought of him as less than a man. He could just imagine how they would treat him if he'd turned the girl down.

Jamal didn't realize it at the time. It was the next morning when the guilt hit him. One of our more experienced tempters (Skeezer) was handling him at the time. Skeezer took great pains to show the young man just how much of a hypocrite he'd made himself. Things were going very well for us until the young, almost Christian had a close call.

Even though he didn't drink, he still went out with his friends on pass. He felt like he should do what he could to keep them out of trouble. In his view, they were his friends, after all. He had been raised to care for those that he claimed as friends.

His group had a privileged young man from a well-to-do family with the surname Ross. Private Ross was a football hothead who was used to being the important person in a group. He didn't mix well in the army, where all privates are just privates. Whenever they went out, Ross would become loud and boisterous, trying to assume the role of leader.

The "leader" brought them into conflict with the locals on more than one occasion. One particular night they were out at the local bar, and Ross was feeling large and in charge. Jamal knew something was wrong when he saw the regulars pulling out their cell phones and begin recording what looked like the beginning of an altercation.

Ross had asked a young lady to dance, and her boyfriend had refused for her. Ross drunkenly explained to the other man that he was asking her, not him. Loud words were bandied about, and Jamal tried to get between the men to settle things down. There was a scuffle with Jamal between the two men.

When the men were pulled apart, Jamal felt a sting in his lower back. He heard a woman's scream and looked down. There was an ice pick handle protruding from his lower back. A flash of pain let him know that he'd been stabbed close to his kidney.

One of his friends screamed, "Call 911!" as Jamal fell to his knees and passed out. He woke up in the ambulance. He was lying on his side with an EMT strapping his legs down. The wound wasn't as serious as it could have been, but it was scary enough.

The EMT just happened to be a devout Christian. I don't believe in coincidence. This was planned by the Creator to snatch this one from our grasp. Years of work went right down the drain as this country bumpkin paramedic witnessed to our young man.

His upbringing came back to him during that time in the ambulance. Jamal realized he wasn't in mortal danger from his wound. He was in danger of losing his soul if he turned away from the Creator. He was aware that he wasn't promised another day of life. Grace was available but only to the living. He realized his mortality.

Jamal accepted the offer of grace from his creator right there in the ambulance. He did so, knowing his own sinfulness. He had the full realization that he could do nothing to save himself and that it was only the grace of God that could save him. In the space of an hour, we lost a soul we'd worked on for years.

Of course, Skeezer was severely punished for losing one that was practically ours. I don't think you will have to worry about him coming back to claim his territory. He is rather indisposed. I suppose he will be indisposed for a long time. Punishment is a useful tool.

Your new charge finished out his enlistment and came home to be near his family. He took a job at a local factory while using his G.I.

Bill to pay his way through college. His mother and father were elated at the news of his conversion. They were doubly thrilled to hear of his decision to move back home and go to school.

Your charge has been without demonic influence for a while now. Usually, we don't assign a full-time tempter to a converted Christian. We usually use them as a training tool because of our shortage of tempters. What is the sense in assigning a full-time tempter to a human who is out of reach? That is where you come in.

Jamal Williams is now YOUR problem. You will do whatever you can to subvert God's purpose in his life. You will do what you can to weaken his faith. As I explained to you from the beginning, we expect results from our tempters. I expect a message from you right away regarding this charge.

Your Infernal Mentor,

Shacklebolt

Master Tempter, I.T.B.

My idiotic tempter, Pinegrub,

I received your last pathetic attempt at a message. You should think twice before you try to bounce ideas off me. Yet, I am not favorably disposed toward you. Why would I give you good advice? You didn't follow my advice before. You paid truly scant attention to the guidance I offered you.

You are to send me messages of how things are going with your charge. You are to let me know how successful your attempts are. You will let me know of your surroundings and your strategies. You will keep me apprised of the weaknesses of your charge. You are not to contact me just to whine.

I will, however, give you this nugget of advice and information. Your charge is a saved Christian. You cannot lead them into damnation. They are saved. The One who saved them is the One who will keep them. Your job is to make them a useless Christian. You are to ensure that they are worthless in spreading the Gospel message.

You are to distract them from their faith. He is saved now and forever. Find his besetting sin and occupy him with it. A carnal Christian is worthless to the church. If you can keep his mind away from his savior, he will be too occupied by the concerns of the world to do his Lord's bidding.

I don't think I need to explain that if you fail in your duties, you will be punished. You personally need to turn this young man into a worthless lump to his God. If you don't apply yourself rigorously, you will find yourself punished far worse than the pain you caused me. I will not try to lessen your punishment or your responsibility. You will face the full brunt of your actions.

If you have any brains at all, you can use the tactics I've already taught you to gather the information you need. If you think that you can contact Grand Tempter Jojun for help, think again. I expressed that you would be under discipline. Even one with his authority would not interfere with the discipline of a tempter. The cost to him would be too great.

You are to follow your charge wherever he goes. Yes, that means even when he is worshipping in his church. You are to stay with him during his times of praise and prayer. Those are the times that are the most crucial.

You will interrupt his prayers. You will plant horrible thoughts in his mind. You will constantly tell him his prayers aren't being heard. You will remind him repetitively of his sins and tell him that God couldn't possibly love him.

Now stop your incessant whining and get to work. I expect frequent reports on how you are doing. I will see some measure of progress from your endeavors, or you will pay the price.

Your Impatient Mentor,

Shacklebolt

Master Tempter, I.T.B.

My Whimpering useless tempter, Pinegrub,

I received your message about accompanying your charge to the Revival Service. The conduct you described is normal for such a gathering. After the songs and assorted praise, the preacher normally stands up and attempts to deliver a stirring and powerful message. The power of the message depends completely on the walk of the preacher giving it. Well, not completely; it also depends on the need of the congregation.

Your description of the burning pain and the smoke streaming from your skin was amusing. The work you are doing is necessary. Here is some of the proof of its necessity. Your communication stated that there were two lower-level angels present at the service. That is a telling fact.

The presence of the Holy Spirit in a gathering of that sort is always to be expected. He resides inside his children, where they go, he goes. The presence of the angels tells you that there are individuals who are under protection or under discipline.

You need to watch the angelic host at these gatherings. It should be easy enough to tell who their charge or charges are. Before you ask, yes, sometimes an angel is assigned to more than one human charge. They are given the power to perform the tasks they are designated.

An angel may be instructed to monitor the conduct of a member of the congregation that is in danger of leading others astray. A Christian who strays from the path can be used to drag others down that same path. Our infernal majesty would be very satisfied if we could render all the Christians useless in His cause.

Do not mistake me. I am not saying that a Christian will lead another to their damnation. I am saying that a wayward Christian can easily be a contributing factor for a person not choosing to follow the Lord. A defeated Christian who doesn't show love but exhibits hypocrisy is what our infernal leader points at to show the uselessness of Christianity.

The world readily accepts this view because they want it to be true. You already know that the fallen nature of mankind compels man to wish God did not exist. When Adam and Eve fell from grace, what was the first thing they did? They tried to hide from God.

It is this wish that God did not exist, that you are to use as a weapon in your arsenal. You are nowhere near as helpless as you seem to think you are. You have the whisper that you were given when you became a tempter. You still have the speed you had as a messenger. Last but not least, you have the aid of their fallen natures. Christians practically scream their besetting sins to us. All you need to do is watch and it will become apparent.

These are Christians, yes, but they are human. They aren't immune to your persuasion. They are resistant to it when they so choose. That is the key. You must use their free will against them. You know all this already. Why are you letting a small amount of adversity in your situation stop you in your tracks?

Their own Bible tells them in James 1:14, that they sin when they are dragged away by their own desires. I taught you to look for their weaknesses. Their weakness will always be what they desire. It doesn't do any good to offer someone something they don't want. If you approach them with what they desire, they will perk up and pay attention.

Watch your charge while you are at church with him. Pay attention to how he reacts, who he talks to, and especially who he looks at. Is there a female that he looks at often? Is there another man there that draws forth his ire? Is there an older person there that won't stop trying to advise him?

I know you are in pain while you are there. I know that you are uncomfortable. You must ignore your physical situation. That is the only way you are going to get through this and make any progress.
You are a demon and a tempter! You are no stranger to pain, and you are already fighting a battle of impossible odds. Gather up your pride and step onto the battlefield as befits your station.

It appears you have another weapon that you aren't even considering. Have you forgotten the almighty cell phone? Does the young man have one? How often does he check his email? Does he use the text function much? Does he have a Facebook account? How about Instagram or Twitter? Is he on a dating website? Start working on the cell phone issue.

He is a single young man. Have you forgotten what human hormones do to their decision-making abilities? Do you remember the amount of trouble you were able to generate for your last charge just because of competition and sexual tension? Just the sex act alone was the catalyst that led to her demise.

I know that there are other tempters around you. Is there a female in the church that he finds attractive? Have they spoken? Is his interest genuine or purely sexual? If you can avoid the former, then, by all means do so. You want to try to tempt him into a purely carnal relationship. In any case, try to get something started between this young man and some flighty female.

Seek aid from the other tempters. You can wreak havoc by having more than one female pursue him at the same time. In days gone by, it was unthinkable for a woman to pursue a man. Times have changed. Some women today are brazen in their pursuit of the opposite sex. Church women are just more discreet about it.

If you haven't figured it out yet, this assignment is a good bit of your punishment. Until this assignment ends, you will be going into churches with praying Christians. That pain should be a reminder to you of who is in charge. You would not be attempting to render a Christian useless if you had but listened.

Your last assignment ended spectacularly. Then like an idiot, you turned on the only one who has been trying to help you. My job is to train you. My job is not to cause your destruction. You allowed a smooth-talking superior with an unfathomable grudge against me to use you. Do you see now who is paying the price? Do you see Grand Tempter Jojun or any of his underlings being punished?

I had intended on finding you a relatively easy charge as a reward for your performance. I had known that something was amiss, but you had gotten the job done. That is all that matters, after all. I was unaware of Jojun's ill feelings toward me.

As far as that goes, some research on my part has turned up an answer. When I was a young tempter, I was working on a particularly difficult charge. One of Jojun's protégés was assigned to aid me in a rather complex seduction. His protégé bungled the assignment and was severely punished. Jojun took it as a stain on his record and held me accountable. He thought this was his opportunity to pay me back.

The Grand Tempter, of course, admitted nothing to me. You will find that the higher you go in our chain of command, the murkier the waters. There have been times that I had no idea why I was given an assignment. I had the good sense, however, to do as I was told and not buck the system.

That is where you failed. You almost cost me my existence. Don't think the softening tone of this message means I've forgiven you. I have not. We, however, have a job to do. We can't very well get that job done with you screaming because you're on fire all the time. I will tell you, nevertheless, before this job is over, you will have more than paid for my pain.

Send me a report on the issues that I've mentioned. I would like you to also send me your impressions of the church. Is the Pastor walking a true walk, or is he wavering? How hard would it be to introduce a female temptation to this man of God? We can probably plant a few wolves into the fold. That is always fun to watch. I expect a reply soon.

Your Infernal Mentor,

Shacklebolt

Master Tempter, I.T.B.

My most junior tempter, Pinegrub,

I received your message and found, to my surprise, that you followed my instructions, for the most part. I believe I've already explained that you need not regale me with your suffering during the church services. You are enduring what you deserve in punishment. Continue to speak on the issue, and I will order you to sit on a new Christian's shoulder during their baptism. That will teach you to shut up.

I see that your young man has a cell phone. You say that he has Facebook but no other social media. I see by your description that he doesn't use the phone other than to make phone calls. We shall have to remedy that. We need to decide on the method of how this can best be done.

Find out if any of his associates use social media accounts. If they do, you can use that as an excuse for him to reach them when calling them is not an option. Since I know, you will ask the question, here is the answer. If he is at work and isn't supposed to make personal calls would be a valid reason. Another would be if he were in a particularly noisy place such as a concert where a phone call would be ineffective.

Snapchat, Instagram, and Tagged are social media programs that we have deep roots in. Try to get him to sign up for any or all of those. We have deep roots in those, along with Facebook and Twitter. There are more, but they are currently small. Our lord thinks big. We can influence what is allowed by the monitors, along with a feeling of privacy and security that we broadcast while our agents are on duty.

This will all make sense if you consider the number of humans caught doing the wrong things online. If you pay close attention, you will see that we only draw attention to the ones who will damage the Christian moral code. We expose the supposed strong Christians when they have clandestine affairs online.

We do expose some of the non-Christian public. That is to keep the public believing that we are non-biased. Why would we bother with the ones we already own? We are trying to damage Christian witness and cast as wide a net as possible for those who remain. We walk a fine line. If we expose too many of our own, then the fear of exposure would be more than they would risk.

At this point, let me restate my desire. I want you to get him as active on every social media account as you can. The next time I hear from you, I expect some progress on this venue. I have given you the answers you need and the means to do it. Don't fail me in this.

You tell me that one of the females in the church has caught his eye. This was the barest of facts. You need to find out who she is. What is her history? Is she a devout Christian? If so, we may need to pass this one by. The last thing we want is for him to grow stronger in his faith. We are trying to undermine it.

If this female is of the carnal persuasion, she is just another reason to get your charge on social media. If we can get the two of them together, we can expose him to her friends. I can almost promise, at least one of her friends will be interested in him. Then we sow the seeds of betrayal and mistrust.

You must find out everything you can about this female. Contact any imps or tempters you see around her. Find out if she has an assigned tempter. If she does, follow her around until you see him. At that point, you need to make contact.

Tell him about your charge. See if he is willing to work with you to bring the two of them into an illicit relationship. If he is any demon at all, he will be open to the idea. If she is already in a relationship, that is even better. We could start your young man out as the other man. That would really sting his self-image.

At any rate, enlist the help of the other tempter. At the very least, use her to get your charge to become active on social media. We can tangle it up later, but for right now, we must get things going.

Your message indicated that he looked upon her with great interest. Was it solely her appearance? I need you to explain to me the nature of his interest. If you are unsure, tell me of his behavior when he looks at her. Where do his eyes linger when he gazes upon her?

Does he look at any particular part of her body? Does he look solely at her face? Does he smile when he looks at her, or does he appear to be in deep concentration? Has he heard her voice? Does she sing? Has he heard her sing along with the congregation, or has he heard her sing a solo?

I am feeding you suggestions on what you need to look for. Remember what I told you about information. The more information you have on your charge and those around them, the better able you are to influence their actions and attitudes. You should be using the things

I taught you with your last charge. You can't have forgotten all of it.

You did very well with your last charge. Aside from the issue of betrayal, you managed things very nicely. I shouldn't have to coach you this closely. I understand that you are unsure of yourself because of being caught. There is nothing you can do now but move forward and try to earn your keep. Don't worry about your punishment. I will see to that.

What is the relationship with his parents? You said he has stayed in contact. I need more than that. Do they talk every night or once a week? Are they enjoying the time they are in contact, or is it merely cordial? Does he seem to desire a closer relationship, or is he going through the motions out of guilt?

Watch how he interacts with his parents. He is a grown man now. He has his own way of doing things. Pay attention to the things that his mother or father say in casual conversation. Use your whisper to sensitize him to their opinions. Try to steer him into believing that they don't approve of the way he does things.

If he is respectful to his parents, he will hold his feelings to himself. He will begin to stew over slights of which they are completely unaware. That is a good recipe to let simmer a while. When he finally works up the nerve to rebuff them, he will be more forceful than necessary.

Something like this can cause a good rift between caring families. I've seen families go years without speaking, all because of a simple misunderstanding. The nectar of that situation is they don't know we are the ones who caused it. If you are successful in this, you will be able to laugh at his expression every time his parents are brought up.

Moving on to the last subject of this message, the pastor. I see by your description that he is a married man. You also tell me that his wife is overbearing and very forceful. You said that he is a quiet man and that she balances him out with her decisiveness. You must be looking at something other than what you described to me.

Your account of the situations you sent me was of a different stroke. A pastor who doesn't actively shepherd his flock is too passive for his faith. Whenever you see a preacher who is allowing his wife to run things, it is time to take notice. The first thing you do is determine if she is taking on the pastor's authority. She is the wife, not the pastor.

I want you to look around at the congregation during the next service. By your descriptions, there are devout Christians there, but that can't be all. I believe you have some agents of our lord in the flock. If this notion turns out to be true, then aid for your cause is readily available.

Keep me apprised of the situation on all the issues I've discussed. Watch the pastor's wife. Who does she talk to? Does she seem to be getting moral support from anyone other than her husband? Tell me of anything that strikes you as odd for a devoted Christian woman.

Your Infernal Mentor,

Shacklebolt

Master Tempter, I.T.B.

My junior tempter, Pinegrub,

I received your communication and must say that I am glad to see you are stepping up your performance. I don't mind the occasional mention of your situation, but nobody wants to hear you drone on and on about it. It is good that you are presenting me with the facts and the barest of references to your discomfort.

I was extremely gratified to read that your surveillance of the pastor's wife led you to a discovery. You describe a meeting with one of the men of the congregation. By your description, this meeting was clandestine, and they were taking some trouble to keep it that way. Did you ask yourself why they met for lunch at a diner two towns away from where they live?

Your message stated that the man was a newly appointed deacon of the church named Stephen Ligans. I don't readily recall why, but that name is excruciatingly familiar. Let me do some digging on the matter. I think you may have stumbled onto something of some import. At this point, I want you to stay away from both of them until I advise you otherwise.

When I tell you to stay away from them, I mean it. Don't ask the other tempters in the area about them. Don't bring them up in casual conversation. Don't ask an innocent question about the deacons of the church. Don't ask about the pastor's wife with any other man. Until I tell you otherwise, this subject is forbidden upon pain of banishment to Sheol.

I see that you have done your homework concerning the young lady that your charge has been noticing. According to your message, she is the granddaughter of one of the church elders. You intimated that she flirts with the faith but isn't serious about it. She is a child of the world. Her parents have not imparted their faith to her.

You say that she is intelligent and possesses a keen wit. Let me remind you that an intelligent person with spiritual knowledge is cause for caution. She may not practice the faith as you say, but if she sees too much of your handiwork, it will point her unerringly to her Creator. If you are not careful, you will cause her to be saved.

Don't do anything aggressive with her yet. Observe her with her friends when her parents aren't around. We need to know her belief in her family's faith. Wait until she is alone with a friend or two. Prompt the friend to point out that her family is very religious.

Then prompt the friend to ask her what she really believes.

This is a quiet way for us to see where she really stands. She may be dancing near the flame, like all adolescents do. They find it exciting to push the boundaries to see how far they can go. The problem for some is that they don't see the danger until it is too late. Then they are ours, and we keep them in despair.

Pay attention to these things when you observe her. Does she flinch or grimace when her friends take the Lord's name in vain? Does she lie easily? Is she a gossip? Does she have a need for attention? Does her world revolve around her, or does she seem to give real thought to the things of God?

What can you tell me of her habits with social media? Does she have one or more accounts? Does she hide her online activity from her family? If she does hide it, find out why. Is it a sincere desire for her own privacy, or is she doing things she knows are wrong? Find out precisely what she is doing. Oh, and one last thing. What is her name?

I had ordered you to make progress regarding your charge's use of social media. I am not happy with your progress. Your activities here are barely enough to keep you from punishment. You will improve in this area, or you will be punished.

You have prompted your charge to be slightly more active on his Facebook account. It does us no good to lead him down a road that doesn't compromise his faith. You were able to prompt him to spend more time on Facebook. That could have been a good thing, but you didn't stay with him while he was online.

He joined a Christian group and accepted several friend requests from people he met in their chat group. You weren't supposed to lead him into deepening his faith! That was the exact opposite of what you were supposed to do.

This situation may be salvageable, however. Just as we have agents in the church, we have agents in the social media groups. Forward me the names of the individuals with whom he has "made friends." We may find that one of them is an agent of ours. If not, we may find a wayward Christian in the lot.

I will contact Jomgrim. He is in charge of our false Christians online. He should be able to point us to several of his agents that can reach out to your young man. Humans are unaware of just how many agents we have among them. A great deal of the human agents we use are unaware of it. They believe themselves free-thinking individuals who are the "captains" of their own destiny. What a laugh.

This latest generation spends so much time connected online that they don't realize they are disconnected from the real world. They are trying to exist in a shadow reality they call the internet. Almost none of them understand that their reality is already a shadow of the true reality that awaits them after they pass from this life.

That is an amusing thought. Their own Bible tells them this very thing. The idea is alien to them because so few of them bother to read the book. Pulling humans away from the word of God has been one of our greatest achievements. Lucifer and his lieutenants find it so amusing. They have the answers to so many of their questions about this life, and yet they refuse to take the time to read it.

I digress. Jomgrim has at least two hundred online agents per thousand of the population in any given city in the U.S. This number is significantly higher than the percentages we historically used. Lucifer feels our time is growing short. For that reason, he has stepped up the campaign of evil. He and his inner circle believe total corruption of the human race is possible.

I tell you this to help you understand, you aren't working alone. We have ample resources to ensure your young man is a useless lump. We can only do this, however, if he is handled properly. You are not living up to your end of this bargain. You need to put aside your discomfort and get back to work.

You also say that you have been able to get your charge to sign up for another email account. Really!? That is your contribution to our cause? At one point, email was a valuable tool for us. Email was used to send secret messages to illicit lovers. It was used to send correspondence for less than legal business deals. That isn't the case anymore.

We have entered the time of real-time communication. Prompt your charge to sign up for one or more of the messenger applications. I have already instructed you to prompt him to sign up for more social media accounts. Do whatever you can to get him to consider the dating sites.

I know there are other tempters in the area. If you don't

understand what I'm telling you to do, then ask a tempter how they do it. It isn't hard to get a human to consider something. Have you been using the whisper at all? It sounds a great deal like you don't understand the gift that you've been given.

I will give you this bit of advice. When you whisper to your charge, make sure it is something they desire or want. Remember that I told you before; a temptation is always something they desire. When you whisper to your charge, try to make your voice pleasant. Try to use your own desire to see them sin to make your voice more seductive.

Tell them how much they will enjoy it. Point out the things you know they like about the idea. Stay away from the negative aspects until after they've committed the sin. It is after they've sinned that you can condemn them. That is when you can tear down their self-esteem and tell them how worthless they are.

We will speak more about this after I receive your next message. I want an update on the girl. Look around and see if there are any other likely females he may find interesting. At this point, I don't care if you find him a nice one-night stand. That would be preferable to his self-imposed celibacy.

Stay away from the pastor's wife! Get me the information that I've been asking for and work on using the whisper.

Your Infernal Mentor,

Shacklebolt

Master Tempter, I.T.B.

My idiotic young tempter, Pinegrub,

What is wrong with you!? I started reading your message and at first, was a bit satisfied. Then you tell me you let your charge attempt to witness to a nonbeliever. You say you <u>let</u> him attempt to witness! You sat by and did nothing!? What do you think you are there for? Did you eat popcorn while you were being entertained?!

IDIOT!! IDIOT!! IDIOT!! You are there to draw him from the faith. You are not there to allow him to find expression for his faith. It only deepens a human's conviction when they attempt to witness to another. For them, it is a scary thing. They are trying to share something that is sacred to them. They are never sure of how it will be received.

His attempt may have been faltering, as you say. It may have been ill-conceived and almost laughable, as you describe it. One thing it was not was a failure. Their Bible tells them that the word of God will not return void. That means that no matter how badly it was presented, the word of God will serve its purpose.

I can assure you that the attempt was looked upon with favor from the Father. IT IS THE GREAT COMMISSION! Have you not been reading the scriptures as I said? Christ gave is disciples this order in the book of Matthew 28:16-20. We are to keep them from sowing the seeds of the Gospel if we can. Sharing the truth makes him happy and proud when his children obey him. The instruction came directly from the Son to his followers.

Just before He ascended into heaven, Christ gave His disciples instructions to make disciples of all nations. That is the great commission. When you allowed him to witness to another, you were allowing him to fulfill his duty as a believer. You did nothing while your charge was obeying the will of God.

I think you know that you will have to be punished for this. Your performance with this charge is far from what it should be. You did so well with your first charge. This charge has so far been your undoing. I want to know what made you think it would be a good idea to just sit back and watch.

It is a travesty that I'm even writing this message. You seem to be so erratic when it comes to temptation. This job isn't difficult when you pay attention to what is going on around you. I am at a loss to figure out what is going on in your mind. If you don't know what to do, then do nothing or contact me!

Don't bother answering this message. By the time you finish reading this, I will be there with two other master tempters. Because of your accusation of me prior to this charge, I must take steps to guard myself. We will be there to demand an accounting of your actions.

Your Infernal Mentor,

Shacklebolt
Master Tempter, I.T.B.

To: His lordship, Third Prince of the dark realm, Premier Exalted Tempter InsidiousDream,

Your Excellency, I find myself on this day required to accompany Master Tempter Shacklebolt. I am to witness and report his actions to you and to keep a record. Along with two other master tempters, He and I go to render discipline to his youngest tempter. The other two master tempters are Master Tempter Slimegob and Master Tempter Wordtwist. I will write the events as they happen to keep an accurate account of what occurs.

We arrived at the residence of the charge of tempter Pinegrub. There was no one about at that time. Master Shacklebolt decided that a search of the home was in order. He wished to know more about the charge, claiming that his tempter's information was woefully inadequate.

Master Shacklebolt found a series of erotic stories in a trunk at the foot of the young man's bed. The stories appeared to be rather worn from folding. Upon making the discovery, Master Shacklebolt uttered in surprise, "So this young man's temptations are of the mind. That will be a bit of help in his corruption."

The other masters were very agreeable to Master Shacklebolt's assessment. They said it showed a lack of motivation on the part of the tempter for such evidence to go unnoticed. They pointed out a slightly erotic figurine on the nightstand as a telltale clue. They also made note of a calendar of provocatively dressed ladies entitled 'Today's Strong Woman".

Master Shacklebolt stated that none of this evidence had been brought to his attention. He intimated that his junior tempter provided the barest of information on this charge. He also indicated that he had expected more from this tempter after such a stellar performance on his last case.

Master Slimegob made note of the smell wafting in the air. He stated that the host of heaven had recently been in the apartment. It was his estimation that a minimum of two low-level angels had been there. From his assessment, they were likely sent to comfort the young man in an hour of testing. He also made note that it was grave news for our cause.

This young man appeared to be resisting almost all attempts at temptation. The fact that the angels had been present indicated that the young man was leading a fairly active prayer life. Master Shacklebolt was most displeased to hear this. He stated that he had categorically ordered Pinegrub to do all that was possible to interfere with the young man's prayers.

Master Wordtwist was amused at this point. He pointed out that all tempters had hidden things from their masters. After a moment, the other two conceded the point. Master Shacklebolt added that still, there was no excuse for letting the situation get this out of hand. The young one could have asked for help.

Master Slimegob came forward at that point. He posed this question to Master Shacklebolt, "Are you going to punish him for his failures, or are you going to punish him out of revenge?" I must admit a certain amount of surprise at the answer that was given.

"In all honesty," Shacklebolt answered, "I suppose some of both, not quite in equal measure."

We stood there in silence for a moment as that answer was processed. Master Slimegob returned, "You know as well as I do that we have the authority to punish and a certain amount of revenge is allowed, even almost expected. But don't go further than you need."

Master Shacklebolt complained that he was not an idiot, and the conversation was laughed away. I did note an eye roll on the part of Master Wordtwist at that point. It appeared that he was on the fence concerning Shacklebolt's idiocy.

The charge came into his apartment at that time. He was being followed closely by the tempter Pinegrub. The tempter seemed to be whispering into his charges ear about Facebook and sending an illicit message. The tempter was quite nervous and didn't seem to understand the ability he was trying to implement.

Shacklebolt rushed forward and grasped Pinegrub by the scruff of his neck. The smaller tempter shrieked in terror when he realized he wasn't alone. He began some babbling apology to his master for his lack of progress while offering the excuse that he was doing his best under a terrible circumstance.

His teacher would hear none of his excuses. He screamed for the tempter to remain quiet. The tempter honestly tried to comply. Only the occasional sob was heard coming from the tempter while Shacklebolt railed against his conduct and lack of progress.

After his initial tirade, Shacklebolt introduced the two other Master tempters. When the other two Masters made an appearance, looking as horrifying as they could manage, the young tempter fainted from fear. All three masters had a jolly laugh at this. They began to discuss rather loudly what they intended to do to the young tempter.

It was that moment when the charge, one Jamal Williams, seemed to sense the presence of evil in the room. He began a spontaneous and sincere prayer to the Creator. The Throne of God answered his prayer immediately. The room was engulfed in blinding light. Heavenly music filled the room, and I felt myself burning.

The pain was incredibly intense. For a moment, none of the tempters nor I could move. Suddenly Shacklebolt roared defiance, picked up his student, and leaped through the wall. His action spurred the rest of us into motion. We all landed in a smoking heap on the ground outside the apartment building.

It took a few moments for our flesh to stop sizzling. When the smoke finally cleared, Master Wordtwist spoke up. He presented the point that what we just went through was obviously why his tempter wasn't making any headway. Given what we had just gone through, Master Shacklebolt could hardly argue the point.

The young tempter found his voice and explained that every time he did anything more than light tempting, his charge reacted that way. He predicted that the young man would be deep in communion with the Holy Spirit at the moment. Master Slimegob levitated to the window and looked inside. He confirmed the tempter's suspicions, stating there was no way to go back into the apartment at this time.

The whole situation seemed to deflate Master Shacklebolt. It seemed he no longer had grounds to punish a lazy tempter. He still had grounds for a dressing down, but that was all. Master Shacklebolt seemed rather angry and almost childish about the whole thing.

Finally, after what seemed like a great internal struggle, Master Shacklebolt turned to his tempter and acknowledged the problems presented by his charge. He stated that this was still no excuse for sloppy work, pointing out the erotic stories and the calendar.

The tempter was genuinely surprised by the revelation and stated that the room was bathed in holy light most of the time. He had assumed that the young man viewed the room as a shrine to his Creator. He did, however, offer a fervent promise to do all in his power to disrupt the young man's prayer life.

Given the strength of the response to the charge's prayers earlier, we all knew the promise was almost in vain. Master Shacklebolt saw no reason to continue with the visit. He instructed his charge to send him more detailed updates, and we left. Master Wordtwist seemed to be enjoying some internal joke but said nothing.

The two other Master Tempters left for their offices while I asked Master Shacklebolt if he needed anything else. He stated a very heartfelt no and bade me leave him to his work. I heard something breaking in his office after the door closed upon my leaving.

My account ends here.

Your faithful servant,

Argass

Junior Secretary, I.T.B.

My least favored tempter, Pinegrub,

Let us admit to the situation as it is. I don't like you. As a matter of fact, because of your betrayal, I hate you. I tried to train you in good faith, and at your first opportunity, you betrayed me. You caused me unspeakable pain and personal violation at the hands of a demon lord.

It is true that in the current situation, you are safe. Your good fortune will not last. You have chosen, however inadvertently, to pit yourself against me. I am a master tempter with more than a thousand years of experience. You have no hope to match wits with me and win. I will see you punished for what you've done to me. When that punishment is done, you will never think to challenge me again.

I see by your latest message that you are still attempting to persuade your charge to become more active on Facebook. Information on the girl has been forwarded to me. From what I've learned from my contacts, her name is Debra Sutton. She appears to be a Christian, but it is only a facade. She is as flighty and worldly as girls her age reared outside the church. Peer pressure has been her downfall. She knows better but doesn't hold her faith in regard.

Her grandfather is an elder of the church, as you say. What you didn't say is that he is a retired evangelical preacher. Fifteen years ago, he led his congregation in a revival that saw hundreds saved. When I say saved, I mean truly saved. It wasn't the "pray this prayer and you are saved" garbage that we see today. You need to pay serious attention to the relationship between the two.

I have arranged for a tempter to prompt Debra to approach your charge. Toward the end of the conversation, she will give your charge her Facebook screen name. She will ask him to send her a friend request. Her homepage has several images of her in rather revealing yet socially decent attire. That should make your young man more active on at least one social media account.

I have also arranged for one of her friends (Jennifer by name) to show some interest in Jamal. Mr. Williams will have a day that will cause him to look at himself with a bit of manly pride. This Jennifer will be prompted to retrieve his Facebook account name. That should be enough of a nudge to get this little love triangle underway.

Jennifer's tempter is a bandy-legged scheming demon named Heeldragger. He has a good bit of influence over her. He assured me that he will prompt Jennifer to ask Jamal to stay in contact using the Tagged application. This will have the added effect of making him much more active on social media.

Soon his cell phone will be the most important thing in his life. These two wayward females will lead him straight into idolatry. He will be led astray by his hormones to worship their attentions and their bodies. This will be the red light for him. He won't even see his phone as a threat.

It is a tool. It is his prized possession. He won't suspect the hold it has on his mind. It will be second nature to take it with him everywhere. It will be nothing for him to check his messages in the middle of a church service. The ding sound it makes will pull him from his evening prayers to check his messages.

If you are paying attention, I just got done in a matter of a few sentences what I've been demanding of you for months now. If you are feeling inadequate, it is because you are.

I received a note from the secretary that came with us to your charge's apartment. Argass was his name. In any event, this Argass confirmed a suspicion I've expressed to you. You seem not to understand the ability you were gifted when you were granted the office of tempter. I will try to explain it again. If this helps, fine. If it doesn't help, ensure that you let me know what seems to be the issue.

The whisper is a will-based power. It is primarily an ability wielded only by spiritual beings. There have been a few humans that were gifted with this ability by our lord. Those people are the ones that will forever go down in history. You may have heard of them. Adolph Hitler was one. Jim Jones and Charles Manson were others.

As I stated, the power is will-based. That means you must desire the outcome you are trying to bring about. The more you desire an action or attitude, the more effect you have on your subject. Simply chanting what you want your charge to do is not enough. You must want it. Set it in your mind to be something that you genuinely want.

If you want your charge to lie to someone, here is what you do. First, you need to realize that telling an untruth breaks one of the Creator's commandments. With that thought firmly in mind, consider that you are attempting to lead one of His children somewhere He doesn't want them to go.

The very thought that you are thwarting the pleasure of the One who threw us away should create the desire in you. As you experience that desire, consider the pleasure you will have when the deed is done. You will have the satisfaction of knowing that by your words alone, you incited disobedience in one of His children. Never forget that one single sin is an offense that damns them.

I know what you are thinking. You are thinking, "My charge is already saved." You would be correct in that, but most of the people around him aren't. Most of the people around him don't even understand what being saved is. Your job is to make him such a poor example of Christianity that no one who knows him wants any part of the Jesus that 'supposedly' saved him.

A Christian who regularly lies is a good example. If a person knows that you can't trust the word of a liar, why would they trust the word of a Christian liar? A liar is a liar. Christian is just a fancy title to put in front of a very condemning word. How many fights have you seen fought over one person calling another that very word?

From this day forward, I want you to practice the whisper in the manner that I've described. If you don't understand what I've imparted in this message, then contact me. Let me know where your difficulty lies. If you feel the need, you know where my office is. I am your mentor, and I have a job to do just as you do.

We move on to the matter of the pastor's wife. You informed me that she was meeting in secret with a deacon named Stephen Ligans. I had ordered you not to do anything at all. For once, you obeyed my command, and it likely saved us both a great deal of trouble. I was curious because of the name and with good reason.

The name Ligans is a Latin word. It translates to "binder." Our lord always uses name meanings for his servants. I believe he adopted that practice from the creator. If you remember your scripture, The Father sent "the destroyer" to slay all of the firstborn males in Egypt where there was no blood on the doorpost. You should know that this took place in the book of Exodus chapter 12 verses 12-13.

The preacher of the church where your charge attends caught the attention of the local demon lord. It seems the preacher was taking an active hand in proclaiming the Gospel and calling others to a higher moral standard. The young lord petitioned Lucifer for aid in the matter. You should know that our lord doesn't do things by half. He sent one of his powerful servants.

Binder is a lower prince of Lucifer. Don't be fooled by the term lower prince. He is still a prince of our realm. His power is such that if he took notice of us with disapproval, our presence on this plane of existence would end. We would both be in Sheol before we could recognize the threat. As I commanded before, stay away from him and out of his way.

From what I can piece together, he is here to neutralize the pastor. It seems he is already enjoying some success. By your description, the pastor has become a passive husband and an almost indifferent shepherd to his flock. If you look at the results of his interactions, you might learn a few things. Don't come into any direct contact with him. If he hasn't noticed you, ensure it stays that way.

At this point, I want you to watch Mr. Williams's online activity. Keep me informed of who he is messaging. Try to disrupt his prayers. If nothing else, try to convince him how lucky God is to have him. That generally tends to work with newer Christians.

Even though I've provided you with more information on Miss Sutton than you knew, inform me the instant you learn anything new. I want information, and you know I will punish you if you don't produce something for me. Now get to work.

Your Infernal Mentor,

Shacklebolt

Master Tempter, I.T.B.

My pathetic junior tempter, Pinegrub,

I received your latest message with almost no hope of improvement on your part. I will have to say that I was not surprised when you expressed that you are having difficulty in disrupting the young man's prayers. You did so well on your last charge. It must be a rather large letdown to perform so dismally in this instance.

A large part of your problem is that your charge is saved. You have less than half of the influence you would have if he weren't. The Holy Spirit resides inside of him. He is already owned by the Father. All you can hope to do is distract him from his mission as a Christian. That mission is to spread the Gospel so the Lord can save souls.

Most Christians have their mission wrong. They mistakenly believe they are to go out and save souls for the Father. That is not the case. Only God can save a soul. A Christian is saved by grace through faith in the redeemer Jesus Christ. You have no idea how painful it was to write that down for you. If I ever have to remind you of this again, I will make you eat the book of Ephesians chapter 2 verses 8-9. Oh, and as an added incentive, I'll do it in a thriving church while sing praises to the Almighty.

We have adjusted tactics in this current age. We have been able to dilute the message to the point of the absurd. We have a huge number of people believing that praying the sinner's prayer once in their life ensures them a place in Heaven.

We have also spread around a good number of false beliefs. We have those who espouse that your life is judged by the number of good deeds vs. the number of bad deeds. If your good deeds outweigh your bad deeds, then you get into heaven.

I know that I have told you it is your job to make him an ineffective Christian. His prayer life is a direct reflection of his walk with his God. When we came with the threat of punishment, we noticed a few things. One of those things is that he treats his bedroom as a shrine.

Here is something you need to understand. Because he treats the room as holy, he is binding a good bit of his prayer life there. Because of this, the bulk of his 'serious' prayers will be offered there. When he kneels to pray isn't the only time he is praying.

As a Christian, his thought life is also his prayer life. That is your way in. Just as you did with your last charge, don't give him a moment of peace. You know he is interested in women. Use that. Bombard him with thoughts of what they may be willing to do with him or to him. Send him images of what they may or may not look like without their clothing.

He is a man. He is young. That means he is at the whim of his hormones, at least part of the time. I haven't seen a young man in centuries that could control himself completely. We already have a clue about what he secretly enjoys.

Mr. Williams had erotic stories in his "Shrine" along with a calendar of "Today's Strong Woman." Use that knowledge to your advantage. Send him dreams of domineering women dressed in armor. If that doesn't work, then send him a dream of working in an office for a beautiful dominating woman.

Keep trying different combinations of these preferences until you hit on one that gets a reaction. You will know it when you see it. His reaction will be rather dramatic. His respiration will increase. His heart rate will suddenly increase. If he is looking at an image he enjoys, his pupils will dilate.

In the end, all I'm telling you to do is, don't wait until he starts praying to fight against it. Work on him constantly. His prayers will be distracted and weak if you have his mind on something carnal. The world has things he wants. We know what one of them is. Now you can use that thing to find more.

Consider how preoccupied you can make this young man. I'm sure that by now, his online activity is starting to distract him from his Lord. A man's desires all too often take precedence over spiritual things. We already have all we needed for our purposes. We know what he secretly wants. That is our toehold into his spiritual life.

One of the human preachers once said, "All the devil needs is a toehold. If he gets a toehold, he'll turn it into a foothold. Then he will turn the foothold into a stronghold." I don't believe he knew how true his words were. That is exactly what we do. We take the small sins in a person's life and inflame them.

You can do this with Mr. Williams. Look around at all that he has. He has a job that is sufficient to pay his bills. He has a roof over his head. He has food to eat. He has a family. What is he lacking? The answer is companionship. That is why he had those stories and that calendar in his bedroom.

He treats his bedroom not only as his shrine but also as his secret place. It seems that he is trying to project that he is fine just the way he is. If that were true, we wouldn't have found anything in his room. We have the breadcrumbs we need to follow. We just need to follow them to the end of the trail.

Part of your problem at the moment is your lack of patience. Remember that we are eternal beings. Humans are immortal from the moment of their conception. The vast majority of them are blind to that fact.

Let's work through a tactic you can use. You are dealing with a saved Christian. You can't cause him to be dragged off to hell. You can only render him useless to his God. You have found that he is active in his prayer life, and he resists your leadings. What do you do?

First, you must identify any weaknesses he may have. We have already done that. We know that he harbors a desire for strong women. His mother was a strong-willed woman. That is probably where it stems from. We also know that he is battling against his desires of lust. We know this because of the erotic stories we found.

You are inexperienced with the whisper, and you really don't have a handle on it yet. You can put thoughts into their minds, but you can't produce the urge to do the deed. You know you must practice but, what do you do in the meantime?

I've always found that a good tactic to use on a practicing Christian is the diversion. As I told you before, you need to keep hammering at him. That at least will confuse his thoughts a bit. But a diversion at the right time is worth a great deal in a temptation.

You have some imps around you. Use them. They are there in the home at your command. When he starts to kneel down to pray, have one of the imps trip the breaker in the bedroom. He will get up to investigate. This will cause him to lose his train of thought.

If you find that he is walking through the house singing a praise song, have one of the imps trigger the fire alarm. I promise you that he will stop singing when that happens. He will think that it is just faulty. He will probably replace it. That will be a good laugh on your part.

Consider this, any time that you can keep him from praying or praising the creator is time well spent. Keep in mind, you can't take him away from God, but you can cause him to wander aimlessly. That is where you need to spend most of your time until you can master the whisper.

There are a thousand little tricks you can arrange for the imps to do for you. Turn off the hot water heater. Disrupt his television signal. Cause static to come through his radio. Warm-up his cold drinks quickly or cool down his hot drinks. You are trying to preoccupy him. A really good one is to cause an itch to occur on his back. He can't reach it. He will spend time looking for something to scratch with. The whole time it will be driving him mad.

Try these things and keep me posted. I want some detailed reports from you about these exact suggestions. I know from experience that they work. Get to work.

Your Infernal Mentor,

Shacklebolt

Master Tempter, I.T.B.

My slightly improving junior tempter, Pinegrub,

I received your message and was gratified to read that the tactics I gave you were effective. I was glad to hear that the imps in the area took direction from you so readily. Did you offer them something? I've never known imps to be so malleable in their nature.

All the tactics that I laid out for you had one thing in common. They were all simple. My old mentor used to say that simple tricks are the most reliable. He was right. They have worked for centuries. The humans never seem to learn to avoid them. If they do learn, they only retain it for a generation or so.

I have been wondering about your behavior. Sometimes you act woefully ignorant of human behavior. You are thousands of years old. You have been a low-level messenger for most of your existence. Didn't you pay attention to the humans while you were in your old profession?

It seems that some of the things you should know, you don't. Almost all of our kind watch the humans as they go about their business. Because of this, we are something of students of human nature. We can guess what their motivations are by their body language or expression. You seem to lack this. Can you give me some idea as to why you have this difficulty?

Upon reflection, in your last case, you followed direction exclusively. You were following the suggestions you were given by the other tempters and me. This includes the suggestions you received from Grand Master Jojun. Was there nothing of your devising in Ms. Bishop's end? I can't help you do your job if you don't tell me what is going on. Keep that in mind when you send me your next message.

At this point, I would like you to continue with the current plan. Always keep one of your imps on him. Have them send him bad dreams. Nothing spoils a human's mood or concentration, like the lack of sleep. If you can keep him preoccupied with concerns of this world, he will be more easily led astray.

Watch your human's behavior closely while he is under your spiritual attack. You will notice something that should seem odd to you. Consider that he is an active Christian. He is an adopted child of his Heavenly Father. He knows about the spiritual aspect of this life. He has an active prayer life. As far as his faith is concerned, he knows what spiritual warfare is. Like ninety-nine percent of all active Christians, he doesn't even consider spiritual warfare a part of his everyday life.

Try this experiment and watch his reactions. In the morning, when he gets out of bed, start blocking all his efforts at least once. If he tries to pick up a cup, cause it to slip from his grasp. Only do each thing once. Cause him to trip once going to his car. Cause him to stub his toe on the couch leg as he goes by.

You only do each thing once because you don't want to make it too obvious. He will be frustrated with himself and wonder what is wrong with him. He will stub his toe and think he wasn't paying the proper attention. He will lose his grip on the cup he is holding and tell himself, "It slipped out of my hand." He won't even think something is causing these things.

When he is praying, have a mosquito or a fly buzz around his head. Cause a dog to bark right outside his window as he prays. Give him a cramp in his leg while he is kneeling to pray. Have your tempters coax spiders into the house. Most men aren't afraid of spiders, but some are. Even if he isn't afraid, they will be a distraction.

This is all aimed at breaking his concentration. If we keep his mind on his worries or a hundred other insignificant things, he won't be praising the one who created him. If his mind is on himself and his problems, he will be much easier to tempt away from the one who saved him. One more time, you can't damn his soul, but you can make him a useless instrument of his faith.

It is important that you make your antics relentless. Push him to the point that he starts thinking he is jinxed or says he has bad luck. Once you have him there, back off just a bit. If you keep him at that point, it is a short step to, "I'm under spiritual attack," and you don't want that.

Once you have him at this level of unwary distraction, bring in your weapons. Use your whisper (that you should be practicing religiously) on the young women. Let them see him struggling with a few things in his life.

Most females have a mothering instinct. When they see a man that they even remotely care about struggling, their heart goes out to them. In their inexperienced young minds, these feelings of support and protectiveness will be perceived as love.

Since he knows that the girls are friends of a sort, he won't tell either that he is entertaining the other. At the early stage, he will console himself with the knowledge that no commitment has been made by anyone. If either asks him directly about the other, he will give very general answers, trying to avoid any promise or commitment.

You will be able to relax your torment of him at that point. His focus will be on himself. He will be consumed with his popularity with the two females. He will experience feelings of pride in himself. He will also experience feelings of self-loathing. He will correctly feel that he is not being completely honest with both girls. But like most men, he will enjoy the attention and will be slow to correct the problem.

This type of situation can devolve rather quickly. If you have contacts with the tempters of the girls, you are going to want to coordinate with them. If, as a group, you do it correctly, you'll be able to keep this going indefinitely. It will depend on how far down the road of falsehood and untruth you are able to drag the three involved.

The girls will be telling themselves that she is the one he is really interested in. It doesn't matter how friendly they were before. Initially, they will feel pity for the other. They will see each other as a rival and feelings of dislike and possibly hatred will blossom. That will be a good kernel of iniquity to keep going in the heart of either of the girls. Always remember, hatred is unacceptable to the Father.

I tell you this by way of telling you what you can expect. I'm not saying that this is exactly what will happen. This is just a general guideline of human behavior in situations like this. It very well could turn out differently, but generally, it doesn't.

Consider your next message to me. I want you to try your best to explain the reason for the shortcoming I've noted above. I'm not trying to find a way to condemn you. At this point, I'm trying to make you a more effective tempter. Remember that as your mentor, when you look bad, I look bad.

In your next message, I want a thorough update on your charge's use of social media. Tell me how much he is using them and to what degree he depends on his phone. We are trying to turn his phone into a shrine in his life. These two females are our way in for this. He sees them as an opportunity, and they are. They just aren't the opportunity he thinks they are.

We will use the females to turn lust and sex into ruling forces in his life. Soon, we will engineer an argument or possibly a fight between the two girls over his attentions. He will then see himself as a lady's man. He won't think of himself as a foolish Christian being drawn from the source of his salvation. If you do what you are told, for now, we will have this dumb human well in hand.

Your Infernal Mentor,

Shacklebolt

Master Tempter, I.T.B.

My slowly plodding junior tempter, Pinegrub,

I received your last message and was extremely pleased. According to your message, you followed all my instructions, and you cleared up something for me. I will admit, I've never heard a story of existence quite like yours. We will need to correspond about this for a bit before we can formulate a plan to use your unique perspective.

You stated that your duties as a messenger were isolated from human contact more often than usual. For over a thousand years, you carried messages back and forth between principalities and princes. Your experience is more along the lines of watching out for and avoiding the Heavenly Host.

Where other messengers are constantly exposed to human contact and thereby observe human behavior, you weren't. You are more a student of angelic behavior. More importantly, you have over a thousand years of observing angelic battle tactics. We can definitely use that knowledge.

In your next message, I would like you to describe what you saw of how the angelic host organized themselves. How did they prepare for battle? Did they seem to have autonomy? Were they strictly, 'We move when God tells us to'? Did they seem to have any individuality in their ranks?

You possess knowledge that could give us the edge in a clash with the Heavenly Host. If you've seen them engage in battles, it is possible that you've seen things that we can exploit. You could be a source of knowledge that demon lords would covet. We may have found an offset to your shortcomings.

Now let's look at the business of your charge. I am extremely pleased with how much use of his social media has increased. I understand that he is using it to keep in contact with the girls. That was the idea. Before we are finished, he will be keeping in contact with just more than these two girls.

Consider what you've written to me about it. You say that he is checking his phone every few hours or so. That will increase as he becomes more involved. The more 'innocent' relationships he has, the more he will be checking his phone. Soon he won't go anywhere without it. He will be checking his phone more than once an hour. Soon he will wonder how he ever got along without the essential technological marvel.

I see that you've made progress on your proficiency with the whisper. I was surprised when you said you just looked back at the other letters referring to how to use that gift. I didn't realize that you were keeping our correspondence as a sort of training manual. That is rather resourceful of you.

You've been able to prompt him to check his messages more frequently. Now you need to work on getting him to post on Facebook. Work on his ego for this. He needs to be of the opinion that all of his friends are interested in what he is doing at any given point in the day.

Your charge is a handsome young man. Use the whisper to send out friend requests to female friends of friends he already has. At least one or two of them will begin a dialogue with him. That will start the snowball rolling. At least one of those will speak of Mr. Williams to Debra or Jennifer.

That is where his reputation as a Christian will start to be sullied. If anything is true among humans, it is "women talk." The girls will begin to compare notes on the young Casanova. By then, lying will have become something of a habit for him. Destroying his credibility as a Christian is our aim, after all.

Hopefully, now you can see how we are going about this. When you are dealing with a Christian, you can't just charge in. You must do it in a roundabout way. Otherwise, an active Christian will have at least one friend who is discerning enough to see what is really going on.

It is up to you at this point to keep whispering to him. Tell him how attractive he is to the ladies. Tell him that he is a catch and that women want a guy like him. Tell him that his jokes are funny, and his conversation is engaging. You must get him to believe how wonderful you keep telling him he is.

This will have the effect of having him consumed with self-interest. He won't consider the things of God while in this state. He will think himself sufficient. He won't consider that he needs God. In the modern language, he will think, "I've got this." This is exactly the opposite of what the Creator intended. He made man for fellowship with Him.

Once he reaches the stage I've just described, he will do one of two things. He will either continue his spiral as a prodigal child of God, or he will repent. The problem for him is that the damage will already have been done. That is the one good thing we reap from tempting a Christian. No matter how much they repent of an action (sin, if you will), someone saw them or was involved. That ruins their "Christian Witness."

I have been meaning to ask you if there are any male companions that your charge spends time with. If he has male friends, we can attempt to corrupt him through them. We can use his peers to exert enormous peer pressure on him. In this current age, being a Christian is viewed as being intolerant. Intolerance is the new unacceptable sin.

Morality doesn't even enter into the argument anymore. This current age is so consumed with "Social Justice" that morality is thrown out completely. It is wrong for one person to have more than another. It doesn't matter that one person works and the other is a lazy sluggard. In the premise of Social Justice, all should have the same.

You can use this topic alone to draw him into worldly conversations and debates. Arguments like this are useless when it comes to getting anything done. Governments that want total control over their citizens offer things like this. If the populace is too fat and lazy to rebel, then the government can do what it pleases. Who would work if all they had to do is sit back and let the government take care of their needs?

The point is that these arguments get him away from the Gospel. The further you can keep him from the influence of the Word of God, the easier your job will be. You can use his male friends very easily in this. Here is how that is accomplished.

Male humans are competitive with each other. You will find a few exceptions to this rule but not a large percentage. It is the desire of young men to be accepted and even admired by their peers. Once a young man has found a social group that "he fits into," that group will have a huge influence on his behavior. It will be his desire to gain and keep the approval of the group.

You can use this desire to draw him away from his God. If you can lead him into a comfortable place in the group, you can make the group his god. He will seek the approval of the group before he seeks the will of his Creator. Suddenly it will be "uncool" to bring up the name of Jesus. When he experiences this, you will have indirectly taught him to be ashamed of his faith. Think of it. You will make him ashamed of the very thing that is saving his soul from damnation. Sometimes the humans make no sense at all. One thing we can say about them, however, they are predictable. Now get to work.

Your Infernal Mentor,

Shacklebolt
Master Tempter, I.T.B.

My more obedient tempter, Pinegrub,

I received your last missive and was extremely pleased and must say a bit proud of your progress. You say that Jamal is now constantly checking his cell phone multiple times per hour. You stated that he is still in contact with the two original girls but has started communicating exclusively through text messages to another young girl he met online.

I'm not all that clear on how they met. You said it was in a chat room. What exactly is a chat room? You had intimated that they met online. Why would they meet online while sitting in the same room? Wouldn't he just look her in the eye and talk to her? Humans are so strange. Send me a more detailed explanation of this.

You say that he is starting to neglect Debra and Jennifer for this new girl. You need to try to counteract this. The busier you can keep him with the three females, the better. You will be keeping him from thoughts of his spiritual condition, and you will be feeding his ego. Just use the whisper to remind him that three females all want his attention. That will do the trick.

Keep in mind that no matter how innocent his relationships with the females stay, we want to sully his reputation. Can you give me any idea how these young ladies feel about our young man? If we can find at least one who has developed real romantic feelings, we can guide both of them to a complete emotional disaster.

One of the things you can count on is that an emotional adolescent human is wonderful for creating havoc. I believe the current generation calls it "drama" or some such. If you can drive your human charge to an emotionally unstable or distraught state, you are playing the real game. This is when they will very readily accept the idea that the whole world is against them personally.

A human-driven to that state is easily manipulated. You can drive them to depression or anger very easily. Just use the whisper to reinforce the thoughts that they have allowed to become ingrained. Tell them their actions are unappreciated. Tell them they don't receive fair credit for their good deeds. Reiterate that no one really cares about them. Tell them that they have no impact on the world around them. Tell them they aren't worth the trouble.

I am looking at the notes I made about your message. Debra has a spiritual background. That made her somewhat dangerous to our mission. Jennifer was a school companion of Debra's. She was a good offset to Debra's spiritual threat. Now you bring in Gloria Jones. At the beginning of your message, you stated that she was very spiritual. I admit to becoming angry upon reading that statement.

Further down in your message, you identify Miss Jones as a devout Jehovah's Witness. My anger completely dissipated at that point. I realize that you've been out of the human loop for over a thousand years. I don't know if you are familiar with our unholy leader's tactics.

One of the things that Lucifer has instituted to draw the Creator's children away is the cults. A cult is a religious system that resembles at least in part the system of worship instituted by the savior. A cult will at least seem to be standing for morality to appear good to the masses.

I know that you are already aware that the best lie always contains some elements of truth. We have successfully influenced humanity to twist Christianity into something more comfortable. No human likes the idea of eternal suffering in Hell. That is one of the common things that happen to "Christianity Light," as Lucifer refers to the cults.

Even though the Bible clearly explains the doctrine of an eternal Hell, human leaders do away with the doctrine. The almost hilarious thing about it is that a huge number of these people accept the changes. They even accept the changes when they can clearly read warnings against those changes in the Word of God. Two references that come to mind are Luke 16 and Mark 9:48.

Human leaders explain away the reasons for the changes, but the bottom line is that they don't want to be accountable to an eternal God. If the doctrine of punishment for the wicked is taken away, then there is no consequence for sinful action. If there is no consequence for sinful action, then the fear of retribution goes away.

Jehovah's Witnesses are one of the faiths that have done away with the doctrine of Hell. In their belief, the souls of the unrighteous are destroyed or annihilated. They also don't believe that Jesus is the eternal son of God. They believe that he is the incarnated archangel, Michael.

One of the hallmarks of a cult is the degree of control that is exercised or sought by the cult leaders. The Watchtower organization uses the threat of being disfellowshipped to control its members. To be disfellowshipped is the same as being cast out of their society. Persons who receive this disciplinary action are to be shunned by all members of the Jehovah's Witness faith system.

The Creator made humankind to be social. Shunning an individual by all others brings a tremendous amount of peer pressure to fall into line. This is a truly effective way to bring wayward individuals back into the fold. You will find that influencing a leader of a group to use this tactic will be extremely useful.

The Watchtower organization claims to receive new light from time to time. For instance, they predicted Armageddon in 1925 and in 1975. Both of those dates have come and gone. The explanation is they have received "New Light" on a prophecy.

In ancient times, the standard for accuracy in prophecy was 100 percent. There was no tolerance for inaccuracy. The punishment for a failed prophecy was stoning to death. If you look around today, you will see that the standard has relaxed to an insane degree.

By that standard alone, the prophecy that Armageddon would occur in 1925 should have been the death blow to the Watchtower organization and the Jehovah's Witness system of faith and practices. If you investigate this, you will find there are millions of JW's (as they are called now). The faith both thrives and expands in this new enlightened world.

The laughable thing about this is that the Bible itself says that God is unchanging. I believe the book of James 1:17 states there is no variableness in God. If God is unchanging, but the Watchtower organization keeps changing its beliefs or system, then how can they be of God?

I tell you all of this to make you aware of an ally. In the book of Matthew, Jesus told his disciples, "Whoever is not with me is against me." Anyone who denies the Deity of Christ denies Christ. You can't deny part of his message. To only accept part of it is to deny the rest. Keep that in mind when you decide who you want your charge interacting with.

Get me more information on Miss Jones. We will have to decide how best to use this young lady. Tell me all about her. Is she pretty? Is your charge especially attracted to her? Have you met her tempter? Is he amenable to working together? Find out who his master tempter is.

While you are gathering this information, give me more of an update on the state of things with the other two females. Does it seem that either of them is tiring of Jamal? How physical have things progressed with either of the other two? I would also like an update on the state of his relationship with his parents. Now get to it.

Your Infernal Mentor,

Shacklebolt

Master Tempter, I.T.B.

My most junior tempter, Pinegrub,

I got your last message and burst out laughing at myself when I started reading it. When I read your explanation of a chat room, I imagined myself coming across as totally ignorant. At least I didn't pretend to know what you were talking about.

I absolutely hate it when I'm speaking to someone, and they try to appear more knowledgeable than they are. You can always tell when someone is talking from their backside. The trick is, knowing when to leave it alone. Here is a hint, if they are of higher rank than you, pretend to hang on every word.

I was at a demonic mixer and seminar one time some years ago. It was given to learn from and to honor some blow-hard demon named Screwtape. Don't get me wrong, he knew his stuff. He was exquisitely knowledgeable on the human condition.

At the time of the mixer, he had already corrupted thousands of souls. The thing that rubbed me the wrong way was his expectance of our admiration. He was in a room chock full of demons. Not of few of those present were demon lords, and he was practically demanding our admission of his superiority.

The scary part about that night was that most of them willingly gave him that admission. I will admit that he was a smooth talker. I will also admit that he knew how to work a room. He had the four largest demon lords in the room practically salivating over his advice.

The thing I didn't like was this. No matter what conversation was going on around him, he seemed to have a need to make a comment. A few times, those comments were almost amateurish. There were a few odd looks, but no one said a word. It was his night, after all.

I believe that he has since been promoted to Grand Master Tempter. The story that I got was that he'd been whisked off to some secret location to train only the best of the best. Sometimes our unholy leader will assign a group of his students to work on a thriving church. More often than not, the church falls because of their attentions. So, there is something to work toward.

I see that you've met Miss Jones' tempter. I don't like your description. In your message, you call him the jovial type. That is not a good thing. Consider that you are dealing with a demon. He doesn't know you at all. What you are seeing of him is a facade that he puts forward as he gets to know you. The nice ones or the easy-going ones are the ones you need to watch the most as you get to know. You will never know where you stand with him until he shows his true colors.

Your lack of interaction with your own kind is a concern that we need to keep in mind. In some ways, you are much like a human child. You trust far too easily. I know that you are thinking, "We are all seeking the same goal." In your mind, we should all be working together. Put that out of your mind. Your brethren will be seeking every advantage they can get. Most demons seek their own agenda.

There are demons that aren't seeking the death of every human. They are considered traitors by our unholy leader. They have the belief that if they help or at least don't hinder humans, their punishment will be lessened. The logic behind their beliefs is, "They didn't ask to be born a Nephilim, so they will cooperate with the Creator as much as possible."

I understand their reasoning. I, of course, don't agree with it. That is a lot like saying, "I know I can't win, so I won't try." It is true that we didn't ask for any of this, but here we are. Losing without a fight is not our way for the most part.

I'm not going to ask you to figure out your own kind. I am going to ask you to inform me before you make any commitments. I will be able to guide you into not making a stupid mistake. You know the kind of mistake of which I speak. You know the kind that causes you to betray and be punished by your master.

I see that your charge has been in more contact with his parents. You say his father is becoming the spiritual mentor that he was meant to be. I don't like the sound of that at all. Are you saying that the young man is becoming more spiritual in the midst of what we are doing to him through these females?

That short description that you wrote me is troubling indeed. We have put in a great deal of work to alienate this young man from his father, and you are telling me they are mending fences. I despise when circumstances take a twist like this. It always seems so unfair to our side.

Here we are dragging these brutes down the path of worldliness and selfishness, and along comes a child of the Creator with the message of forgiveness. They croon out the message, "Your Heavenly Father forgives you out of love, but He also requires that you learn to forgive those who harm you out of love as well."

The very thought makes me nauseous. I was there along with hundreds of our brethren when He spoke. He said, "Father, forgive them, for they don't know what they are doing." Some of us thought he was talking about us. For a fleeting moment, the multitude of demons were confused. His last words made no sense to us.

Then the fallen lord screamed out the meaning of the Redeemer's plea. We went insane with rage. There was a demonic riot. The thought that we had played into the Creator's plan drove us mad. Many of the demons present attempted to kill the humans around us. A huge bolt from Heaven scattered us at the same moment the Redeemer breathed his last.

The shockwave from that bolt tore the veil of the temple in two. The lot of us didn't know what that meant at the time. The gateway between God and man had been thrown wide open. With the same action, our destruction was driven home to us. There would be no redemption for us. We had already passed from mortal existence.

That is enough of this reminiscence, on to more pressing issues. You say that Mr. Williams views Miss Jones with a sense of wonder. He sees her as passionate about her faith. He finds her attractive both physically and spiritually. That is an excellent combination. We can use this.

Has your charge mentioned Miss Jones to his parents? You are going to want to keep them apart for as long as possible. Work with her tempter to keep her busy on any day that a visit would be possible. Do the same with the group of tempters working around his father.

We don't have a tempter that is particularly effective against his parents. They have armored themselves in the full armor of God. We can't allow Jamal to reach that stage if we can stop it. At the point he learns to put on the armor and keep it on, we will lose almost all influence on him.

You will need to use the whisper to highlight all of the things he finds attractive about Miss Jones. Call special attention to her innocence. Every young man likes to think that he is the first in the eyes of a young lady. By your descriptions, the chastity of Jennifer and even Miss Sutton can be called into question.

We are going to undergo a shift in plans at this point. I know we were trying to turn him into a ruthless man about town. That won't work at this point. He is drawing closer to his father. We have to strike while we still have time. Use all your influence to aid him in developing feelings for our little she-wolf in sheep's clothing. The beauty of this is that she is completely sincere. She genuinely believes in her faith, and that is what makes her all the more dangerous.

You will have to centralize his attention on Miss Jones. See about ending his associations with the other two. They are useless to us at this point. We are going to try to draw him into a false faith, and we need to do it before his father finds out what is going on.

Let me know how things go in your attempt to draw him to her. Keep me informed of any offers made to you by her tempter. Don't make any commitments without my advice. Do what you can to draw him away from the influence of his parents. Keep them apart as much as possible. You have your assignments; now get to them.

Your Infernal Mentor,

Shacklebolt

Master Tempter, I.T.B.

My more obedient tempter, Pinegrub,

I must say that I am much more satisfied with this message than I have with any other since you began with this charge. You indicate that the ties between the two other females have been severed. I find it amusing that you say they were severed at a cost to your charge. That is always the case when a young man ends any type of relationship with a female.

You indicated that he was able to sever any type of relationship with Miss Sutton rather cleanly. It would seem her interest in him had waned over time. However, Jennifer was a bit more upset at the breakup.

It appears that Jennifer was a bit more invested in the relationship than was suspected. By your description, she had developed genuine feelings for the young man. Your descriptions of their encounters didn't describe physical involvement as yet. Are you sure you haven't neglected to inform me of anything?

I found it amusing when I read that she physically damaged his car. You said it was called "keying" his car to damage the paint. How did he react to this? Your report indicated that he was surprised at her reaction. Considering his relative inexperience with relationships, I'm sure that Jennifer's reaction was a great shock. I was just wondering if he physically threatened her.

I will say it does appear that females in this time period have much more of a "take charge" attitude when their feelings are involved. This could be only cultural influences bringing about this change. A woman wouldn't dream of such assertion a hundred years ago. Five hundred years ago, a woman would have meekly accepted the man's proclamation.

Your report stated that your charge called the police and then changed his mind. You stated that he did this several times until the police traced the call and contacted him. They inquired as to the reason for his multiple hang-ups. Then they explained that such behavior on his part was against the law and chargeable.

It was at this point that he apologized for his behavior and explained the reason for his calls. The police asked if he would like to press charges against the young lady for vandalism, to which he said no. The law enforcement officer then advised the young man to handle his problem without further involving them.

Now you must admit that it was fun to cause such mischief. Wasn't it novel and exhilarating to work with Jennifer's tempter? You stated that he had his claws in her skull while whispering to her of the indignation of this "skinny goofy guy" dumping her. The spiritual discomfort of the claws and the prompting of the whisper was all that was needed to send her over the already precarious edge.

Keep in mind that while the endeavor was successful, it is not a cause for you to trust her tempter. He is a demon. Like you, he can't be trusted. Yes, I said like you. I don't trust you, Pinegrub. I will never forget that you betrayed me on your very first mission. You would do well to remember that I have not exacted my full vengeance for your treachery. Now, let's get back to the subject at hand.

Always remember that humans are much easier to control when you have them emotionally off-balance. The Creator designed them to be creatures of love driven by conscious thought. Conscious thought is where free will and choice come into play. Luckily for us, their emotional stability was skewed out of kilter in the fall from grace.

I assure you, if you play your cards right, this won't be the last of Miss Jennifer. All her tempter has to do is keep grinding in the thought that "He had the nerve to dump her. Who does he think he is?" Those two sentences will be enough to aggravate her sense of pride for the near future. They will also be enough to cause your charge a good bit of grief and distraction.

I especially enjoyed the portion of your report that dealt with Jamal's parents. You explained that Jamal met his father at a coffee shop on his way back to his apartment at the end of his shift. His father thought one on one time with his son was necessary for mentoring him in the faith.

It was a simple matter for you to instruct the imps to disable Pastor Williams' car while they were inside chatting. It was only a loose wire, but that was all that was needed. The imps wouldn't have been allowed to affect much in any event.

Pastor Williams' key fob had no effect when he tried to unlock his car. That was enough to keep Jamal from just getting in his car and driving off. After looking under the hood and not being able to find a problem, Pastor Williams gave up.

He called a tow truck and asked Jamal to give him a ride home. Being concerned for his father, Jamal didn't remember that Miss Jones had left her Bible in his car. They both got into the car without a thought. Pastor Williams saw the Bible and opened it, with the remark that Jamal carried two Bibles.

That was when the fun really started. It didn't take long for the Pastor to discover that the Bible was a New World Translation. Jamal tried to defend Miss Jones while his father declared the Jehovah's Witness faith to be apostate. I have to say that I loved the description you used of their disagreement.

These are the times that really add zest to our work. We were able to negatively affect the lives of Christians. The best part is that neither of them, even the experienced Pastor saw our part in it. They didn't see all the work we did to set it up.

In situations like this, we are using the Creator's own inventions to our advantage. Jamal loves his father and wants to believe in a lifetime of teaching. He has investigated the truth of his faith and genuinely believes. Your young charge knows his father is sincere and honestly desires to share the love of God with everyone.

On the other hand, he is very smitten with Miss Jones. He finds her attractive on a physical, mental, and spiritual level. He feels a connection with her that he hasn't felt with others. He believes she is truly sincere in her beliefs, and he admires that about her.

He knows that he is facing two opposing views. He understands that they both can't be right. At this point in time, he feels rather trapped. No matter which path he chooses, he is going to lose someone important to him.

This type of situation is what the Redeemer was referring to when he said, "If anyone comes to me and does not hate father and mother, wife and children, brothers and sisters - yes, even their own life - such a person cannot be my disciple." This appears in their scripture in the Gospel of Luke, chapter 14 verse 26. It would be in your best interest to memorize the passages I give you.

At any rate, almost none of these monkeys seem to understand what he was talking about. He didn't mean you have to hate your family. He meant your love for him should be so great in comparison that following him in your mind should be automatic. A believer shouldn't worry about what others do or think at all. They are to let their Lord handle problems of that nature, and they worry about their own behavior.

Now the Pastor is worried about losing his son again. The son is seeing his father in a very intolerant light. Neither is making any attempt at seeing the other's point of view. The most delicious part of it all is that neither is considering the will of their Creator in any of this. Watching something like this unfold in the life of a believer is like drinking nectar.

At this point, we want to keep as much turmoil going as we can. Ask Jennifer's tempter if he is agreeable to keep that little fire going. While he is doing that, see if you can get Miss Jones tempter in on the fun. Ask him to prompt Miss Jones to intolerance of faith's that in her view are pretenders. Ask him to pay special attention to her view of "Christians."

While they are doing this, ask a pair of your imps to shout to Jamal's parents. Since they can't get very close, they can scream discouragement from a distance. It may work. It may not. Let's see if we get lucky. Make sure they shout things about the son leaving the faith and how Pastor Williams was a bad father. He is our main target in this campaign.

You, my bad demon, will be using your whisper to demoralize your charge. Tell him how his father will never accept Miss Jones. Tell him that Gloria is a loving person, and it's not her fault she was brought up in an apostate faith. Whisper words like tolerance and perseverance to him. Try to impart the idea that if he shows her the way, he may be able to save her.

This is the same tactic we use on the spouse of an alcoholic or addict. You would be shocked to see how many humans will stay in a bad situation while we feed them that exact line. It is amusing to watch them line up to accept abuse, thinking they are helping out of love. In truth, they are only enabling someone lost in sin.

You have your instructions. Keep me well informed. We have a lot of irons in the fire right now. Let's not lose control of this situation.

Your Infernal Mentor,

Shacklebolt
Master Tempter, I.T.B.

My more successful tempter, Pinegrub,

Finally, you send me a report that sounds like it comes from a competent tempter. It appears you are starting to understand how to keep all the balls in the air at the same time. I must commend you (however reluctantly) for how you've handled your charge and those around him.

It was entertaining to read about the tension between your charge and his father. Pastor Williams, being a Southern Baptist preacher, tends to be rather unforgiving of those faiths that are seen as a mockery of Christianity. Jamal was hoping for a more open-handed attitude from his father, only to be disappointed.

This is one of the things that you will have to keep going where you can. Most of those who are in the Jehovah's Witness faith are sincere people who genuinely want to serve the Lord. They aren't aware that they've been drawn into our net. We want to keep things that way. So as a tempter, it is up to you to continue the propaganda.

There is different propaganda for different portions of society. For the Jehovah's Witnesses, our aim is for them to believe they are the true faithful. In their view, they have latched on to the truth and must hold on to it tooth and claw. The jaws of hell await them if they fall from the faith.

The propaganda used on a follower of Christ is that they must not fellowship with those in a false faith. They must believe that if they do this, they risk falling into a false system. They should believe that it is best not to even try to bear witness to these poor fallen fools.

The propaganda used on a human that doesn't practice a religious faith is simple. We convince those people that religious people are crazy zealots. If they have any belief at all, we tell them that God is a loving God and there are many different paths to heaven. To this group, we always paint Christians as Bible-thumping hypocrites. It is human nature to dislike a hypocrite, even though all humans are hypocrites to one degree or another.

If the non-believing human has questions of a spiritual nature, we steer them toward a "learned person" or someone we already have in a false faith. The learned person is usually someone with more than average education. They are also someone who can argue a logical point in a worldly manner.

Have you noticed that the false faiths have very rigorous programs to reach out to who they believe are lost? The Muslim faith believes they must spread Islam to non-Muslims. The Jehovah's Witnesses have a strong door-to-door ministry. The Mormons, or as they are referred to now, the Church of Jesus Christ of Latter-Day Saints, have an aggressive missionary program.

We continually work to have all faiths accept each other to one degree or another. The only faith we denigrate and call out as intolerant is the Christian faith. A good number of humans are aware of this, but most of them are ours. If any of them start making noises to the effect, we simply call them intolerant in a very public way.

You probably think I've gotten sidetracked. No, I haven't. As your mentor, it is up to me to teach you what you are supposed to be doing. You seem woefully unprepared for this line of work. I am imparting wisdom to you that you would do well to remember.

Back to the work we are undertaking. You indicated that Jamal's father is becoming more forceful in his condemnation of Miss Jones. Your charge would be more inclined to listen to his father's words if they weren't directed at the young lady. The imps have done a good job in their screeching.

Jamal's father has transferred his displeasure at a false faith onto the object of his son's affections. This will not end well for him. His son sees the girl as innocent. The boy has his eyes on the girl and not the faith she follows. As long as he sees her as an innocent sincere young woman, we can keep this going.

The father's mistake was not putting his faith in his Creator. He sees his son spending time with this woman as a failing in his parenting. He isn't seeing his son as a grown man making his own choices. He is pushing his son to decide before he is ready.

I have heard from the imps that Jamal's mother is giving this problem to the Lord through prayer and fasting. She doesn't seem to be in the limelight of the problem but, she is doing the most about it. She is the one we need to throw off the track. The Creator loves to answer the prayers of His humble saints.

I instructed the imps to start paying special attention to her. I don't know what good it will do with only two imps. I am making the decision to send three more imps to their home. I will instruct them to station themselves right outside their bedroom window. They are to screech out worry and hopelessness, especially to the mother. We can only hope to find the chink in her armor. This woman seems to be putting on the whole armor of God.

We have the son and the father running in circles about this issue. I don't know how long we will be able to keep this up with the mother's prayers in the background. We need to roll out some more issues to take the attention of the men. Hopefully, we can bring them more at odds with each other.

You haven't mentioned anything about Jennifer causing any more mayhem in the young man's life. You need to get her back in the picture. She could add some spice to his life while causing his father to believe his son might have some loose morals with the ladies.

You did say that there was a new female in your charge's apartment building. Was that a mention in passing just to keep me informed, or do you think we could cause some havoc with her? Is she attractive? Has she spoken to Jamal at all? Do they see each other in passing often? Do you think you could engineer a chance meeting?

Remember that no matter how many women you have in a man's life, you can always make it worse by adding another. Have you seen this woman's tempter? What do you know of her other than the fact that she is a female?

This is a possible venue for us to pursue. You need to find and speak to her tempter. Find out what you can about her. Don't make any deals with her tempter. Let me say that again. Don't make any deals with her tempter until you talk to me first. I will tell you when it is alright to strike a bargain with another tempter.

So here is where we are now. We need to be proactive against the mother. We are currently playing the men of the Williams family like a couple of harps. Jennifer needs to be stirred up to take some action against your charge again. There is a new female in Jamal's apartment building that you need to investigate more thoroughly. Finally, we need to see if we can cause interest between Miss Jones and your charge to deepen into something more.

You already know the help you can count on from me. You need to initiate contact with the tempter of the young lady in the apartment building. You also want to speak to Jennifer's tempter to see if you can work together to cause a mutually beneficial incident between the two.

I will be checking in with the imps to monitor the mother. If you need to do anything special, I will let you know. Right now, she is praying and fasting. That is bad enough. Hopefully, we can keep her in a passive role. If she decides to step between the father and son, she could undo a good deal of our work.

You know the situation, and you have your instructions. Now, get to work.

Your Infernal Mentor,

Shacklebolt

Master Tempter, I.T.B.

My nervous young tempter, Pinegrub,

I received your message and must say that I am unsettled with the news you've provided. You have described the Holy Spirit moving in the life of a believer. I don't like this at all. By your description, this happened the night the imps informed me they were ejected from the property of the Williams' family.

They described it as an intensely bright light accompanied by a feeling of togetherness. It made them deathly ill. They were thrown from the property to land in the trash bin of the nearest neighbor. They can no longer shout from the window. They can't even cross the property line, let alone get close to the house.

Your useless complaint that Jamal and his father prayed together garnered no sympathy from me. I know it burns when the Holy Spirit joins with Christians in their prayers. I've experienced it. I know far better than you the violence of being ejected from an area. So, don't cry to me about how it takes so long for the burns to heal.

It seems that things are unraveling on us a bit. Your news that Jennifer is uninterested in causing further strife to your charge was unwelcome. I had thought she was vain and proud enough for at least a couple more altercations. Your news that "She is too mature for the child" does nothing for our plans.

I suspect that her tempter has found richer temptations for her and, further work with your charge would endanger that. You really can't blame him for watching out for his own interests, but it is unfortunate for us.

It would seem that your last message carried even more bad news. You met the tempter for the new neighbor. Your description of him as a "burned out husk" was rather graphic. I did not like reading that the new neighbor is a devout, born-again Christian. You said her tempter was assigned to her as a punishment for a failure. Interesting tactic, don't you think?

Jamal and his father are speaking in civil tones again. I knew that would happen. I was just hoping for some time to corrupt some part of the young man's faith. At the very least, I had hoped to cause a divide between the two. Now we are back to trying to deal with the father truly being a spiritual mentor to his son.

Your news that Jamal admitting that Miss Gloria Jones follows a faith that Christians believe is false was not surprising. We knew the young man's upbringing. It was inevitable that he would come to grips with the fact. All we could hope for was a certain tolerance to take root in his heart. That would have rendered him useless in his faith toward the great commission.

This presents us with a problem. Miss Jones is a devout Jehovah's Witness, and we want to keep her that way. We do not want this young man who cares for her to show her compassion while he witnesses to her. The way we keep these humans in a false faith is to alienate the Christians against them where we can.

This tactic has proven itself time and again. We have our tempters whisper to overprotective elders in the faith. They whisper that the new in Christ are weak and vulnerable. Most of the time, if the elder falls for the whisper, they warn the new Christian away from witnessing to someone in a false faith.

They believe they are protecting the young Christian. They don't realize they are hindering the great commission. It shows a lack of faith in the Holy Spirit of God to protect those he has called. In that instance, we hinder the budding faith of a new Christian and curtail the great commission. That is as much of a win as we can hope for when dealing with Christians.

There is the possibility that Jamal could, in his compassion, plant a seed of doubt in Miss Jones' mind. Of all the things we want for her, we don't want that. Doubt is all that is needed to cause her to research her faith for real. We want her to say to herself, "My father told me.." and "My father wouldn't lead me the wrong way.."

Remember what I told you about the Jehovah's Witness Church using disfellowship to bludgeon their followers into line. The fear of being ostracized by the only community that you have ever known is too much for many people to bear.

You need to speak to her tempter. Inform him of this development. He needs to get all the help he can muster. He will need to call in aid from the tempters of her entire family. They will need to find out about Jamal, not as a potential convert. They will need to see him in the light of a devout Christian.

It is unfortunate that so many of our well-laid plans have come unraveled. We have no choice other than to withdraw and formulate new ones. This is one of the hazards of being a tempter to a Christian. You will need to stick to your charge like glue from this point on. I don't care if he is in devout prayer and it burns like fire. You WILL stay with him.

You will do what you can to try to confuse his prayers. You will try to whisper to him about how controlling his father has been. You will whisper to him that maybe, just maybe, Miss Jones can be saved. It is a true statement, by the way. She could be saved by the blood of the lamb.

While you are whispering to him that she could be saved, continue to whisper tolerance to him. Tell him they are worshipping Jesus after all. Jesus is the Christ. Doesn't that make her a Christian of a sort? Remind him that she is strongly devout in her desire to follow God. Isn't there some way they could meet in the middle?

None of this whispering will do us any good in the end. What it may serve to do is take his mind off the great commission. We don't want him to see her as an unsaved person in need of his compassion. We don't want him to realize the real desire of the Father that this is one of His lost sheep. We don't want him to remember that, first and foremost, he is a Christian.

If we can accomplish this, it will buy us time. That will be time for us to find another chink in this young man's armor to exploit. Your messages indicate a young man who likes to talk to others. He believes he is in pursuit of the truth. Perhaps we can guide him into gossip. That is always a useful detour for a Christian.

If we turn him to gossip, we can let him keep his lofty idea of the truth. We can have him running to and fro for years in the belief that he is only trying to help his fellow Christians. It won't take long to get him addicted to the feel of learning those dirty tidbits of truth about his fellows that no one else knows.

Watch for a time that he is in a conversation about a third party. Pay careful attention to how he reacts. Is he enjoying the conversation? Is he enjoying receiving the nasty little secrets? Does he want more of the same? If the answers to those questions are yes, then you need to look at this most important question.

Is he hiding his enjoyment of it from the person he is talking to? Watch how he phrases the questions he asks. A good gossip masks their curiosity with Godly concern. They use remarks like. "I'm so concerned for sister So-and-so." Or "I'm so worried about brother What's-his-name." That always brings out the innocent question,

"Well, whatever for? Then the gossip begins from there.

I'm not saying he will make a good gossip. I'm just saying that it is one of our possibilities. We have to keep every option open at this point. Use the whisper to nudge him in our intended directions. Let me know of your progress.

Keep him away from the new neighbor. We need more time to fray his faith and fuzzy up his beliefs. We need to really make him ask himself what the truth really is beyond his belief in God. If we can keep him asking questions that he won't get an answer to, we've effectively done our job.

You have your instructions. Now go muddy up the waters. Cast some doubts. Plant the seeds of discord toward Jamal's mother. Try to make him more sympathetic toward Miss Jones. Finally, see if we can sidetrack him into being a gossip.

Your Infernal Mentor,

Shacklebolt

Master Tempter, I.T.B.

My slightly more able tempter, Pinegrub,

Your situation is taking a turn for the better. I was quite happy with the news about Jamal's mother. Your message indicated that you requested a touch of aid from a tempter in the neighborhood. I have warned you more than once not to trust your own kind too easily. Mark my words, this will cost you in some way.

I can't argue with the results of the favor given, though. One of the stay-at-home moms living close by has formed a friendship with Mrs. Williams. You said the young mother is very needy. That is a wonderful thing. Mrs. Williams is getting used to an empty nest. This new friendship will demand a great deal of her time while it is forming.

If we are going to turn this to our advantage, you will need to provide more information. Did you think you could just put the two ladies together and let them graze like two old cows? It doesn't work that way, Pinegrub. I know you are inexperienced, but you need to try to think things through.

Your message stated that this woman was unsaved. That is all well and good, but we don't want to provide the other side with a ready-made convert. You didn't even give me the woman's name! What have you found out about her? You told me her children are of school age. Now that school has started, she has a great deal of time on her hands. She is therefore feeling rather useless.

Before we go any further with this situation, send me all the information you can glean about this woman. What is her name? What are her vices? Does she gossip? Does she swear? Does she lie easily? How is her relationship with her husband? Does she see him as attentive, or does she have a wandering eye? Does she smoke? Does she drink? Send me everything you can find as fast as you find it.

Let us now look at other matters for discussion. It would seem the mother's influence has lessened slightly. You need to stay diligent. This will only be the case for as long as you can keep the mother occupied with the other lady. Talk to the other woman's tempter. See if he is amenable to exposing his charge to the mother. The mother represents a danger. Don't be surprised if he is unwilling.

Jamal and his father are spending more time together. His father is still berating him about Miss Jones. You need to find something to draw his father's thoughts away from the issue. What you need is something that will raise alarm bells even more than false teaching. His father is what they call an old-fashioned Baptist preacher. We need to concentrate on something that will positively horrify the man.

I had a glimmer of a memory of something you wrote. I looked through some of your older messages and found something of note. Last month you reported that a new employee on Jamal's production line is gay. You said that Jamal stayed away from the man primarily out of religious phobia.

This will be the way that we throw his father off the track of Miss Jones. It's hard to be afraid of a growling dog when a roaring lion is in the room. You will work on prompting Jamal to form a friendship with this man. You will need to cloak it in guilt to get the whole thing started.

When you are sure that Jamal is paying attention to your whisper, remind him of the great commission. His Savior said that he is charged with making disciples of those around him. That includes everybody with whom he comes into contact. Remember to tell him that the Savior said, "I have not come to call the righteous, but sinners to repentance.

I know what you are thinking. You think I'm encouraging you to help your charge fulfill his Christian duty. No, I'm not. Your charge is already saved. He is in no way prepared to witness to anyone of this nature yet. He will blunder that part of it. All he will accomplish is giving this man more armor against these hypocritical Christians.

The thing that you will be doing is trying to form some sort of friendship or relationship between this man and Jamal. His father will see it as his weak Christian son falling further into apostasy. The young man already consorts with false faiths, and now he is communing with the residents of Sodom? It will be delicious.

Give Jamal the tiniest understanding that he needs to sincerely befriend this man before witnessing to him. When the friendship takes root, Jamal will have a hard time dealing with the thought that this otherwise nice man is bound for hell. Try to persuade Jamal that he shouldn't offer any condemnation of the man's lifestyle <u>at first</u>. This will cause a feeling of betrayal when Jamal finally broaches the subject of salvation with this poor lost soul.

Jamal will see his father as even more narrow-minded. His father will see him as an ignorant young man who won't listen to reason. It will be the burr under the saddle of their relationship.

Here is what you need to watch out for. When the friendship first begins, do your best to keep Jamal from explaining his beliefs about homosexuality. He would then come across as reasonable and understanding. We don't want that. When Jamal feels comfortable enough to witness, we want his friend to feel like it was all an ambush tactic.

Causing incidents like this is the most effective way to drive the lost away from the Savior. We generate a feeling of judgment and unacceptability in the unsaved. Then we whisper that a loving god wouldn't have made them this way if it were wrong. We try awfully hard to keep them from seeing the love and concern for the lost. We keep the eyes of the lost on themselves and their actions. They don't understand that it isn't about them or what they've done in those moments. It is about what was already done for them on the cross.

I think that is enough of this line of talk. I know you need to understand the why and why not but explaining it in this much detail makes me rather ill. You would do well to remember that I'm only saying this to you so that you will understand. This message would not cause me trouble if you forwarded it. It would make you look like a fool for needing this degree of explanation.

So here is where we are. The mother is hopefully being sidetracked. Don't bet on that though. Still, you need to do all the shouting that you can. Any urges you can implant in her, the better off we are. Try to make her disposed to helping the neighbor.

The son and the father are starting to experience more friction, but hopefully, our plans will amplify that. You will need to check with Miss Jones's tempter and explain what we are trying to do. He can possibly put a spin on it from his side and draw his charge further from the savior.

Understand that you are asking him to expose his charge to the Gospel of Jesus Christ. The fact that he has been willing so far is amazing. He is going to want something in return. Keep that in mind.

Your Infernal Mentor,

Shacklebolt

Master Tempter, I.T.B.

My prematurely elated tempter, Pinegrub,

I received your message about the accident. You are gloriously happy at the death of your charge and his father. You stated they were in the father's car, going to a men's meeting. The drunk driver crossed two lanes of traffic and struck their car at seventy miles per hour. You prattle on about how their influence for the cause of Christianity is done.

At the beginning of your message, you stated that could prompt your charge to reach out a nonjudgmental hand to his gay co-worker. You said you were also able to encourage him to express his feelings for Miss Jones. You said he also did this in a very passive way.

You don't understand where this leaves us. More, in particular, you don't see where this leaves you. You seem to hold the belief that I share responsibility for your failures. Please allow me to attempt to explain the situation as it is now.

We will start with the mother. This faithful Christian woman has lost her husband and their finally restored son. This woman is resting in her faith in God. She genuinely believes she will see her husband and her son again in Heaven.

As a mother, she is assured that her saved Christian son is safe in the arms of their Savior. She believes and is assured of the same fate for her loving husband. She is grieving, but she is grieving their loss from this life while she celebrates their fate.

She was the pastor's wife. Her congregation will rally around her. Many of them will marvel at the faith this woman shows. The evidence of her faith is all around her now. Her testimony has gone from strong to devastating. The Holy Spirit will use her as a beacon to draw more into the faith.

I know you are thinking that she is suffering. Yes, she is, but her suffering has a purpose, and she knows it. She will suffer for a time, but it will pass. Her testimony will impact hundreds or possibly thousands. This is the digital age where her story will go seemingly everywhere, almost instantly.

We must resign ourselves that the Lord will use this situation and this mother to bring Himself glory. This woman will be used to sow the seeds of salvation. The terrible part in this for us is that many will answer. Some of them will indeed fall away, but we can't stop it. The word of salvation will go out, and this woman will be the center of it. We may be looking at a time of revival.

Your job was to protect your charge in a situation like this. Now we have two dead martyrs on our hands. Instead of a lukewarm Christian with an indifferent track record, we have the example of a good Christian father mentoring his son just before their untimely death. A death, I might add, was due to a driver under the influence of alcohol.

The drunk driver only serves to make them that much more of note. They will be heralded as two wonderful human beings who were cut down in the prime of their lives by the demon of alcohol. You weren't around during the time of prohibition. You don't know how hard we worked to make alcohol a socially acceptable substance in America. You don't realize the harm your inattention has wrought.

There is no longer any social tolerance for the driver who has had one or two too many. The courts have increased the penalty for this infraction. The insurance companies and the medical industry campaigns against the overuse of alcohol. While not considered morally evil by the world at large, it is considered a social evil.

You have no idea the amount of work it will take to smooth this over. There will be social outrage that must be handled. We will have to identify the Christian individuals who may take up the fight for this. There will be prayer meetings that we will have to monitor. We will have to pay close attention to the Heavenly Host.

Their actions will be a direct reflection of the will of the Creator concerning this. The tempter who caused the other driver to drive in their inebriated state won't be the problem. He probably won't even be punished. Your side of the equation is where all the possible problems come from.

You potentially had years to wear down your charge's faith. You could have made him the worldly Christian that everyone points to and says, "If that is Christianity, I want no part of the hypocrisy." You could have easily had him doing things that he preached to his friends were "of the devil."

Now, that opportunity is gone. Who do you think is going to get the blame for that? I can assure you, young tempter, it won't be me. I have documented proof that I've been working hard to prepare you. I have proof of your betrayal and of your general ignorance. I also have proof that I've advised you on matters of which you should already be aware. When the higher powers review this blunder, I will be safe.

Your description of the events of the accident was wildly inept. Did you even know what you were looking at? When a child of God dies, angels escort them into the presence of the Most High. At the time of their death, they were completely beyond your reach. Why you tried to use the whisper on your charge as that point is a total mystery.

Your message stated that "as the dust settled, a huge trumpet sounded, and a crack appeared in the air." That was the Savior opening the door to Heaven for His children. The "large crowd" of angels you described was a company of the Heavenly Host serving as an honor guard. Your charges father was a faithful preacher of the Word of God.

You stated that as they left the wreckage, they both saw you. They looked at their broken bodies and then examined themselves. Your charge looked at you accusingly at first. Then his expression softened. That was his realization of his death and your part in the attempted corruption of his faith. You said his smile was like the dawn breaking on his face as he looked around at their angelic escort.

The father broke into spontaneous songs of praise. The commanding angel approached and bowed to him. The father tried to bow back, but the angel stopped him. You said you saw the lips of the angels moving, but you couldn't hear what they were saying. That is because you weren't meant to hear it.

You described how they both looked at each other, and your charge said, "mom." They were expressing concern for the one they were leaving behind. You intimated that the angel then said something else, and their faces eased. He was assuring them that all was as it should be. He was also likely telling your charge that his mother would be fine.

The low booming sound you heard next was the voice of the Lord welcoming them into His presence. You couldn't understand it because you have never been one of His. We, as demons, can't perceive the things that are strictly of God.

The excruciating burning you felt was the direct presence of the Holy Spirit. What in the world made you try to stay in the area at that point? Do you realize now that you were trying to stand in the presence of God? You can't do that! I'm sure, given time, your eyelids and ears will grow back.

That last sonic boom you described just before you were thrown several miles from the area was probably the Creator ordering you to leave. I saw the trench that your body dug out upon impact with the earth. I understand that the local authorities are calling it a meteor strike. Those idiots! Don't they know a meteor inside the atmosphere is called a meteorite?

You are to stay where you are until our lord decides your fate. You may think that lying in the dirt with two broken legs, one broken arm, the other arm ripped off, and the outer layer of your skin burned off should be punishment enough. I say with a certain degree of satisfaction, you are wrong.

I will tell you; I'm going to ask for a piece of you. Your blunder is of such magnitude that I may be granted as much as a whole leg. We shall see. It has been a long time since I savored such a morsel. You are probably lying there thinking, "This is so unfair.", and you would be right. One more time, I will inform you, we are demons. Fair is not part of our vocabulary. Oh, by the way, don't worry. Whatever they take, or give me, will grow back, given time.

Your Hungry Mentor,

Shacklebolt
Master Tempter, I.T.B.

To: His lordship, Third Prince of the dark realm, Premier Exalted Tempter InsidiousDream,

Your Excellency, it is with great satisfaction that I pass on one of your servant's gratitude. A few days ago, you honored the request of one Master Tempter Shacklebolt. It seems you granted him permission to sup on the leg of his junior tempter. The up-jumped imp failed mightily to neutralize the faith of a child of the enemy.

This inattentive bungler failed to guard his human against harm. He allowed the death of his charge and that of the charge's father. The father was a devout preacher for our enemy. You were quite livid when you were informed. As I recall, you granted the request and took the other leg for yourself.

The Master Tempter Shacklebolt offers his most loyal and obsequious thanks for your indulgence. He informed me that the limb in question was a sumptuous repast after being braised with human despair and lightly sprinkled with a baby's tears.

He expressed enthusiastic support of your rulership and stated his desire to aid your Highness in any way possible. I informed him you were in a meeting and not to be disturbed. He appeared exceedingly relieved as he reinforced his support of you. He left after stating that you may call upon him at need.

Your faithful servant,

Argass

Junior Secretary, I.T.B.

My now more educated junior tempter, Pinegrub,

I have not received a message from you for some time. I know you must wait for your legs to grow back, but that is no excuse for laziness. I assume you are still pouting concerning your legs. Let me say that you can be proud that something of you brought satisfaction to your superiors.

I was able to stretch out the morsel I was given for three full meals. I have to say you are very tasty with a light braise sauce. It would be in your interest to strive for success more diligently. I've heard that our lord enjoys far more than just one sampling. There are rumors that he almost nightly enjoys the delicacy of demon flesh. Perhaps you will take to heart the advice you've been given. We are demons. We are not known for our gentleness and caring. Keep that in mind in the future.

It has been a few weeks since the disciplinary action that removed your legs. You were placed in the basement of a highly active Christian church. The burning you suffered during that incarceration also stunted the regrowth of your legs. You have since been removed from the church to nurse your wounds in the local park.

I have very fresh memories of the scorching that occurs to our flesh when believers offer true worship. If I recall correctly, and I'm sure that I do. You were the direct cause of my discomfort. You may have some idiotic idea that we are, as they say, even now. We are not. You may as well scrub that thought from your mind. We are demons. We never settle for being even when provoked.

You need to remove the naïve ideas that plagued you when first we met. We do not exist in a universe with anything like justice for our kind. We will win this war, or we will burn. Think about that for a time. There is no plan B. Even if we win, our place is far from secure.

Consider what we are. We are the product of the union between angelic fathers and human mothers. It was jealousy of the humans that brought many to rebellion. Do you think we will be considered in a favorable light when all is said and done? We could very well be a tool to be used and thrown away. If our well-being were taken into consideration, would you not have both of your legs right now?

While you contemplate this, I want you to think about what you saw when your charge passed from this life. You saw the enemy collect two faithful souls. You survived that encounter only because you were of no consequence. Imagine what would have happened had the Creator desired your destruction. Our battle is avoiding that confrontation.

We are trying to bring the Word of God to ruination. If we can thwart His will even once, we win. The humans don't realize this. They think that the will of the Creator is malleable. It isn't. Everything that He has decreed must come to pass, or He is not Almighty God. If we can break His plan anywhere, we dethrone the Creator of everything. His creation will no longer be under His absolute authority.

By this time, you realize I paint a far darker picture than you received in your initial briefings. In your indoctrination into the tempter ranks, you listened to all the motivational talks about how easily we can win. Those talks were for the naïve fools who can be led to believe we have a good chance at success. We do not. From a true perspective, our lot looks rather grim, even if we win.

At best, we will be second-class citizens in the new regime. At the very worst, we will burn for eternity along with our superiors. I know what you are thinking about this. You think that you didn't ask to be born or to exist. You are thinking that it isn't fair for you to come into existence facing such horrible circumstances. It isn't all about you. Well, there you have it. As the humans say, "It is what it is."

Now, with that out of the way, let's get on to business. Your next charge is one Carlos Rodriguez. He is the oldest child of Rosa and her now late husband, Guillermo Rodriguez. The boy was twelve years old when his father was killed in a construction accident. He attempted to step into his father's shoes as the "man of the house." His parents tried to raise him as a devout Catholic.

Carlos absorbed a good bit of the doctrine of the Catholic faith. He prays to dead saints and bows down to idols. The young man believes in the power of the priesthood to absolve him of his sins. He also believes in Mary as the mother of God and the co-redeemer of humanity. Like most of his generation, he believes his behavior doesn't matter if he says an "Act of Contrition" prayer before he dies.

You will find him rather malleable. Like most youths of his age and culture, he has inherited the vices of temper and pride. He has fallen in with a gang in his misguided attempts to provide for his family's financial needs. His size and ferocity have ensured that he isn't at the bottom of the gang's hierarchy. He has been in several fights for position inside the gang. He has won all of them, with the last two producing some rather bloody results. He hasn't killed anyone yet, but it appears to be just a matter of time.

A gang member in the city can't build a reputation without generating some legal troubles. Indeed, your charge did not start any of the fights that he has engaged in. He did, however, cause serious bodily harm to those who have attacked him. That is a good thing in the gang hierarchy. Legally speaking, it is a bad thing when there are witnesses.

The legal trouble started when your young man soundly defeated an attacker in front of his attacker's girlfriend. The young lady took it upon herself to call the police and swear that her boyfriend was attacked. The resulting court case was heard by a judge with whom we have some influence.

This was a case where we have two tempters coming at problems from different angles. We couldn't give both tempters what they wanted. The attacker's girlfriend needed to be drawn away from the Gospel. In that sense, we needed to give her some sense of vengeance. She affected the revenge, not some ineffective prayer. We were able to give her a sense of power over her life. Her attention once again turned inward instead of to the Creator.

Your charge was a different story. Carlos had been riding high on several successes. It was thought that he could lose this one in a small way without jeopardizing his status. The judge found in favor of the attacker but only sentenced Mr. Rodriguez to weekly counseling. Counseling is a soft punishment for effectively doing nothing wrong. That is the extent of your charge's legal troubles.

Carlos is a young man with a young man's appetites. He has found an attraction to another gang member named Maria. She is the type of female who wants to be with someone prominent who will take care of her. She sees Carlos as a rising star and plans to ride on his coattails until something better comes along. Her last so-called love interest is currently serving ten to twenty years in federal prison for a variety of offenses. One of those offenses is manslaughter.

One of the things I have noticed in perusing this report on your charge is his sense of family. He is very dedicated to his mother. He almost desperately wants to live up to her expectations of him. That is amusing since his becoming a gang member has gone against most of what she has taught him. They are at odds over this subject.

You need to widen that chasm. Whisper to him about how overbearing and impossible she is. Recruit a couple of imps to shout at her about how unruly and disrespectful he is. It should take only a short time for this to influence their relationship. You will love watching two people who love each other hate themselves because they feel abandoned by the other.

She is aware that the only reason he has joined a gang is to provide for the family. She knows that he doesn't agree with the beliefs and practices of the gang. She understands that her continued berating is driving him away. However, as a good catholic, she can't remain silent. He is her son, and she must point out where he is going astray.

He is aware that she is only doing what she is doing out of love and concern for him. He feels compelled to provide for the family and therefore, must disobey his mother. He agonizes over breaking the commandment to honor his mother.

The leader of the gang is Julian. The brash and confident man is also a distant cousin of Maria. That has afforded her a certain amount of status and protection. That protection and status are dwindling of late. Her cousin has observed her behavior and doesn't approve. The gang leader is also a threat to Carlos. He sees your charge as possible competition.

That is the extent of the information that we have gathered on your charge. It is in your best interest to take a few days to observe his behavior, his surroundings, and his interactions. You may find things that our operatives missed. I am sure you know by now that most demons do the bare minimum to get by. That is a good deal like most modern-day Christians.

That is all we can cover without more information. Pay attention to the things I've mentioned and get back to me with your own observations. Keep me apprised of the relationship troubles with the mother.

Your Infernal Mentor,

Shacklebolt

Master Tempter, I.T.B.

My stupidly obstinate tempter, Pinegrub,

I received your message late last evening. It would seem your petulance concerning your punishment is driving you to act out a bit. Don't push your luck too far, young demon. Remember this last punishment. You should not be eager for more. I expect more timely information from you. I won't say this to you again. I will just ensure you are most excruciatingly punished for your attitude.

I see that you have indeed confirmed the friction between mother and son. You stated that you enlisted the aid of three imps to torment the mother. You have them alternately telling her she failed as a mother and that her son is a rebellious, unruly man child.

That will be effective in the short term. Consider that she will grow immune to that much torment over time. Remember that she is sensitive to these thoughts now. She will become callous to these ideas, requiring more heinous tortures for the same result. It is much like human addiction. The addict continues to need more of their drug of choice to achieve their desired high.

I am not saying that the woman will become addicted to the torments you have laid out for her. They will always affect her to one degree or another. Over time, however, she will get used to the idea of always being there, and it won't bother her as much. If you continuously keep up the torment, you are almost doing her a favor in helping her get over it.

What you need to do is find small things that irritate her. Make those things the bread and butter of her daily torment. Once, or possibly twice in a day, make mention of the thoughts you know truly torture her. Make it a weapon that you pull out only to bludgeon her with during an altercation with her son.

Watch her habits to see what she is fussy about. Does she put the dishes in the cabinet only in a certain way? Is she picky about the cleanliness of her home? Does she iron her laundry or just hang it after it dries? Things like this are the things you need to know to truly distract and torment her.

I've seen humans get into huge arguments over which direction the toilet paper rolls off the roller. I once was able to cause a woman to divorce her husband because he ground his teeth in his sleep. They had been married for years. He had done this all his life. She had known it and was unbothered by it at first.

That changed when I drew her attention to it. When I kept whispering to her that it was a sign of uncaring disrespect. I kept telling her that he ground his teeth because he found her intolerable but wasn't man enough to put it into words. I was able to cause several relatively strong arguments between them with that.

I had the imps attacking his sense of manhood the whole time I was working on her. They had him believing that she was trying to dominate him because of something he couldn't control. He was correct, of course, but their insistent chattering at him put him on the razor's edge for a confrontation.

It all came to a head one night when I was able to prod her into striking him with a pan while he slept. I just kept telling her he was taunting her in his sleep. She stared at him for a while and went into the kitchen and got a pan. When she hit him, he woke up and reacted violently. He came out of the bed swinging. His punch landed, and she was slammed against the wall from the force of it.

She called the police and had him taken to jail. The next day when the truth of the matter came out, he was released from jail with the charges of domestic violence dismissed. He went home, packed his things, and moved into a motel.

He promptly put the house up for sale and filed for divorce. She had a change of heart when it was pointed out to her how unreasonable she had been. She had, however, pushed her husband past his endurance. He rebuffed all her attempts at reconciliation, and the divorce was finalized.

I really enjoyed tearing apart a Godly home. I don't think either of them attended church after that. The husband told that Pastor to take a flying leap when he suggested that he forgive his wife. The wife was so embarrassed by her own behavior that she couldn't face her friends at church anymore.

I know that they both secretly missed each other. When I was reassigned, I left them in a state of hopeless confusion. They had no Christian witness in their community. Neither of them had a taste for the counsel of God from their church. The last I heard, they were both very bitter and useless Christians.

That is the type of thing I want you to do to your charge. Find the little things that bother him. When I say that, I mean you need to stay on the alert for such things. You never know when he will be introduced to something new. It is during those times that you will find the new things that drive him up a wall.

I have been watching your charge of late. In my observations, I've noticed a tendency that he absolutely hates to be interrupted. He will listen to another person when they speak without interruption. Because of this, he feels deeply insulted when someone talks over him while he is speaking.

You can capitalize on that. I don't know if you've noticed, but modern cell phones have about a two-second lag from the time a person speaks to the time the sound comes out on the other end. It might not seem like much, but two seconds is a lot of time to work with in a conversation.

Watch and see to prove it to yourself. A human can say most of a sentence before two seconds is up. All you must do is have your imps work on his most talkative companion. Instruct them to chatter about with a sense of urgency in speaking. This will cause them to be more eager to take part in the conversation.

After a short time of their prodding, you will be surprised at how ready they are to break into a discussion. That doesn't mean you have been sitting on your laurels. While the imps are doing their jobs, you are to prime the pump as they say. You will need to whisper to him about how disrespectful it is for people to just cut him off.

Your whisper will make him much more sensitive to the issue. The one who disrupts his normal discussion will soon learn not to do it. The one who does it on the phone will always have the time lag as a defense. He won't really have a reasonable argument for it. He will stew in his anger and resentment.

Remember what you learned in your training. An angry human is easier to control than one who is calm and centered. You will begin to understand, angry is just a blanket term. What you are looking for is keeping your charge emotionally out of balance. If he is out of balance emotionally, he will always react to a stressful situation with confusion.

Your instruction, for now, is to implement the techniques I've outlined for you. I want a report covering this soon. Now, get to work.

Your Infernal Mentor,

Shacklebolt

Master Tempter, I.T.B.

My less than subtle tempter, Pinegrub,

I received your missive and was concerned about your tactics. I realize I am the one who told you to use the lag time on his cell phone as a weapon against his peace of mind. I also realize that you are trying to implement my instructions. It would seem you are not paying attention to the result of your work.

By your description of his actions after your torments, he is using his cell phone less and less. That is not the result we want. As I have explained to you before, the cell phone has become an idol in modern society. If you use it to torment him overly much, he will turn from it. You never throw away a good weapon.

You must moderate how much he is tormented with the time lag against how useful and captivating his phone can be to him. You've already seen that most modern humans check their cell phones at least two to three times an hour. You should understand, they do this because it makes them feel important in their own mind. "I am the center of my own universe" is the thought behind it.

Don't worry, this is not a dressing down. I am merely instructing you concerning nuance and detail. When you torment in a particular area, you should always pay attention to how their reactions will affect your temptations. Temptations are only useful to us when they are desirable. Once your charge is soured on a temptation, we lose a valuable weapon.

This strategy toward temptation comes from our enemy's book. You will find it in the book of James. As you should know, James was the half-brother of the savior. I have not asked you this before, but I will now. Have you read the Bible? If you have not, then you should. You may consider it required reading BEFORE you message me again.

The Bible is the handbook for living a good human life. It contains the words of God to guide humans in their actions. I know that reading it is distasteful for our kind. It is, however, the best source of counter-tactics available to us. When you read the instructions on how they should behave, remember they are fallen.

Instructions on how they are supposed to act means their nature pushes them in the opposite direction. That is an excellent place to start when you want to understand human nature. Once that understanding is gleaned, you watch your charge and find where he or she falls inside that framework. It makes your job much easier.

I assume I've given ample explanations and examples for you to pay attention to this tactic in the future. What we need to do now is guide him back to his love affair with his cell phone. The easiest way to do that is to have his cell phone reward him. A human always pays attention to the things that provide him treats and rewards.

I have spoken to one of our operatives that manages a cellular sweepstakes in the area. We have arranged for your charge to win a sum of money. I believe the sum to be five hundred dollars. It isn't a huge sum, but it is enough to get his attention. It will make him thankful that he had his cell phone. That should go a long way toward bringing his devotion back to his little idol. Keep me informed on this issue.

Another useful tactic is to draw his attention back to the cause of his ire. He hates to be interrupted. You have been using the lag time on his phone to accomplish this. Start using it a couple of times a day in normal conversation. Cause one of his cronies to use it to aggravate him. Don't use it enough to cause a fight. A good fight is too valuable to waste. Fights are for moments of change.

Now on to another issue. I noticed that you haven't given me any information at all on Maria. Does she hold your charge in thrall? Is there anything going on between them? Does Julian enter the picture here? Has he warned her away from Carlos? Has Carlos sensed something and has created distance from her?

We went to a great deal of trouble to put her in his path. I would hate to think that all that effort was wasted. If you can keep her preoccupied with controlling him, a good bit of the battle will be won. He will be so busy resisting her dominance, he'll never be aware of you. She will, in essence, do your job for you.

Have you seen any special animosity from Julian toward your charge? The research that we had identified him as a loose cannon. Our source indicated that he wasn't averse to removing competition. He doesn't have to have proof. He merely needs the suspicion that a threat to his position exists.

You will want to post at least one imp to watch him. You need to be aware of his plans toward your charge. You can't very well have liiiu kill Carlos without your knowledge. Remember what happens to tempters who allow their charges to die on their watch? This was not to bring up a bad memory. This is to keep you aware of your situation. The bad memory was just a bonus for me.

While you are attempting to keep track of all that is going on around you, don't let his Catholic roots slip your mind. You have all that you need to keep your charge from saving faith. He is already entrenched in faith that, by its very actions, sets it against the Creator's commandments.

Remind him that a good Catholic goes to confession. When you persuade him to go to confession, prompt his honesty. Support his belief that no matter how horrendous his sins are, a mere man can absolve him with the words, "I absolve you of your sins.". Let him believe that a few prayers to dead saints cleanses his soul.

You can indulge yourself by letting him get into an argument with a Jehovah's Witness or possibly a Mormon. In them, you have sincere individuals who have been thoroughly misguided. In the three groups, you have people digging for gold where there is none to be found. The most rewarding thing you will find about it is that a good number of them genuinely want to serve God.

The issue for these people is that they want to serve God in their own way. God is not ordered about by the will of his creation. He has provided a way that they refuse to recognize. A large percentage of them refuse out of loyalty to family. They can't abide that the mother or father they loved so much may not be in Heaven. In that way, they are placing their parents above God. Their loved one has taken the place of God in their life.

Do not, and I repeat, do not let him get into a debate with a Christian in your machinations. Aside from letting him die prematurely, we absolutely do not want him exposed to the truth. There is a good chance we can snatch away the seed before it sprouts, but better safe than sorry. The last thing you need is for your unsaved charge to get saved on your watch. There would be no protection for you then.

In closing, implement the instructions I have given you here. You may feel free to variate them a bit but be aware that you will bear the blame should you fail. Keep me informed.

Your Infernal Mentor,

Shacklebolt

Master Tempter, I.T.B.

My up-and-coming tempter, Pinegrub,

Upon reading your latest message, I am happy that you are taking steps to spark new life into his love affair with his cell phone. I see he hasn't won the sweepstakes yet. That will seal the deal for you. Now that you have him using it again, the win will cause it to become more valuable to him.

I will alert you a couple of days ahead of time for the win. If you play your cards right, you can create a strong need for money in your charge. Cause him to overspend on something. That can cause a need for ready cash. You could also whisper a sense of desire to him for something he sees in a catalog, magazine, or flyer. You could more likely do that with something he sees on television.

Television is the great re-programmer that lord Lucifer promised us it would be. We used the influence of television to slowly alter the values of the human culture. What was unthinkable before television is commonplace now. Before television, divorce was almost taboo, and teen pregnancy was an unthinkable embarrassment. Now they are both simply accepted with minor attempts to correct the issues.

People who proclaim themselves Christians watch their language. These same Christians will watch television shows where the Creator's name is used to curse someone. The language on television in its' infancy was strictly controlled. Slowly, according to human time, we introduced more and more foul language.

We now have such freedom with language on television that the F-bomb is commonplace. That is amusing by itself. The Creator's name can be used as a curse without an eyeblink. However, the same audience gets more uncomfortable using the F-bomb to show contempt or denote a sexual act. We have been phenomenally successful using television to devalue the Christian faith.

We are doing the same thing with cell phones. In their infancy, cell phones were bulky creations, affordable only by the rich. Now they are sleek creations by comparison, with a great deal more versatility. There is more computing power in a handheld cell phone than there was in the computer that controlled the moon launch.

By contrast, television service was free once a person owned one. You just plugged the television into an electrical outlet, and you could watch whatever was presented by the networks. Our gradual control over the networks increased over time, giving us more control over the ideas that we presented to the mostly ignorant masses. The humans didn't even suspect that they were being conditioned and programmed to accept morally wrong ideas.

The cell phone was a significant leap forward. It could be carried around by an individual. That made it perfect for placing so much emphasis on oneself. The technology became an idol in the hands of the masses. That idolatry is the very reason the god of this world used government-funded programs to get a cell phone into the hands of those who couldn't otherwise afford them.

I reinforce all of this to ensure that you understand that the cell phone is one of your most powerful tools. You can divert your charges attention with a simple text message that was prompted by an imp you control. If you work in concert with your imps, you can almost completely control your charge.

Here is an example. Your charge dotes on his mother, despite their rocky relationship. His father was a strong male role model that imparted high expectations of his son's behavior. Carlos respected his father greatly and seeks to live up to those expectations because of that respect. Here is a situation you could use his inner expectations against him.

Your young man is approached by a practicing Christian. This is a man that he has gotten to know and respects to a degree. The man broaches the subject of salvation and Carlos's eternal destiny. Carlos believes the Savior is the Son of God by his upbringing. This is a conversation you don't want to go past his admission in belief.

At that point, you direct one of your imps to whisper, yell or screech to Carlos's mother to call her son. It doesn't matter the reason the imp gives. It can be a call for help in the current situation. It can be construed by her as a feeling that her son was in danger. What matters is that she calls him.

His phone rings, and he sees that his mother is trying to contact him. His strong sense of duty compels him to answer the phone. He may excuse himself. Depending on the situation that you have generated, he may be lured away from the situation. The point is that you have effectively used his cell phone to keep the Gospel from him.

That is enough examples and possible scenarios. Let's explore the situation in the gang. The gang to which your charge belongs has a great deal of influence over his life. We have explored what Maria can do for us. We have also spoken of Julian. Don't forget that you have an entire group of worldly humans at your disposal to further corrupt your charge.

The member of the gang that occupies the lowest rung on the hierarchy ladder is Daniel. He is the youngest member and has only been in the gang for just over a month. He is thin and not particularly athletic. He is extremely intelligent and rather cunning. These are qualities that Julian finds important. He is trying to lead the gang in a way that emphasizes intelligent action instead of emotional response.

I would recommend that you use imps to whisper to Daniel. Influence him to befriend Carlos. He is the lowest, so he will have to use flattery and a bit of hero worship to get it done. Whisper that he can promise your charge, he will keep an eye on Julian. If you can, encourage him to befriend both men with the same promise.

That will appeal to Daniel's cunning nature. He will see himself as a double agent who can't lose no matter who comes out on top. Ensure that you don't mention anything about his punishment, should either man discover his duplicity. Should he think overlong on Julian's reaction, he might consider the risk too high.

Find out who is acting as Daniel's tempter. You will need to contact this demon and try to form a working relationship. You both are after the same outcome, damnation for your charges. You don't have to be friendly toward each other to work toward a common goal. Do not trust this individual. They will be seeking an advantage over you the entire time you work together.

You will need information on Daniel's activities to help you control Carlos' attitudes and actions. You will be able to implant certain suspicions in your charge that will prove to be true. This will cause him to trust his "intuition," namely you. This will lead him down the path of trusting whatever you tell him. A charge is easier to control this way.

That is enough for you to work with for now. Heed my warnings given here or proceed at your own peril. I will implement his sweepstakes win on his cell phone. Contact me with any news.

Your Infernal Mentor,

Shacklebolt

Master Tempter, I.T.B.

My most inexperienced tempter, Pinegrub,

I must admit to a certain amount of frustration upon reading your latest message. I found the whole affair a bit choppy. I realize you are trying to follow the letter of my instructions, but I don't need so much meandering details. I don't care what Carlos had for lunch unless it evokes a negative emotional response. I also don't care what Maria was whining about unless it grated on your charge's nerves.

You are giving me minutia. I am looking for ammunition to use against your human whelp. The humans usually go about their day in a haze of "Me.. me... me.". Those are the moments we want to encourage. If he isn't doing anything objectionable to our cause, then leave him alone.

Let him ponder how wonderful HIS world is. It's all about him. That is how the human mind works. They are creatures of self and always will be. All they truly know is what they can see, smell, hear, taste, and touch. This is one of the main things that hinder them from stepping outside of themselves. They never truly see things from the other's perspective.

The only time you will see a human attempt to see from another's perspective is in an emotional battle. When a husband who genuinely loves his wife is told how she feels, and he feels convicted by it. Moments like that are the only time they can step outside of themselves. Parenthood is another place where they tend toward this behavior, but a good dose of selfishness squashes that.

I don't know what possessed you to give me a minute-by-minute account of your charge's day. I don't believe I've asked you for that much detail in the past. Is there something going on that I need to know about? If there is something you think I should know, then tell me. We don't want a repeat of your last deplorable performance.

I did see that the sweepstakes win did exactly what it was supposed to do. I am gladdened to find that Carlos and his phone are inseparable. You might want to see about introducing him to a new online dating site. It will occupy his attention, make his phone more important and reinforce his self-centered lifestyle.

I know you think he has Maria to occupy that aspect of his life. You need to understand, nothing gets a young man's attention like the attention of the ladies. He will be "buying his own press," as they say, when he has the attention of multiple ladies. The hilarious thing about it is this. He doesn't have to meet or even see the women he is communicating with. He only needs some interaction with them. Try this one out, and you will see that I'm speaking the truth.

I think I now see the reason for the idiotic format of your last message. You say that Daniel's tempter is a demon named Slagheap. I know this one. He is a total idiot. We went through tempter training together long ago. You seem to be adopting some of his advice. Don't!

Think upon this. He is a junior tempter like you. How is that? He has been a tempter for hundreds of years. Why hasn't he moved up in the ranks? I will tell you exactly why. He is too fearful. He won't take a chance at all. He is far too afraid of punishment to achieve anything.

He is the type of demon who whispers and cajoles. He never tries to impress his will on his charge. In his view, that would be tantamount to announcing his presence. That would still be his attitude if he were the tempter of a Satanic priest. He is far too afraid and cautious for his advice to be anything for you.

You still need to take what information he shares with you. I would dare say that you could probably gain an advantage over him, but that would sidetrack what we are trying to do. So here is a brief instructional order. Get what information you can from him. Gain contacts from him if you can. Don't take any of his advice on how to handle anything. I mean anything!

You did ask a worrying question in your missive. You said the gang has allowed a new member to join. You stated that the young man is named Amir and is of Arabic descent. You indicated that he is of the Muslim faith and asked if you should keep him away from Carlos. That brings me to a question.

I know you've had precious little contact with humans. When you were assigned as a tempter, you had to know you would be tempting humans. Did it occur to you to do any research at all about human society? Have you researched anything to do with human religion?

In this instance, I'm not just going to give you the answer. I expect you to do some research on your own. I want you to find out what you can about the Muslim faith (and that should be a great deal). In your next message, I want you to answer your own question and give me the reason for your answer.

I realize you are inexperienced, but you won't learn if you don't do the work of finding out. You have ways of finding out things without resorting to asking me everything. Think of your situation and consider what might be a good source of human information. Then consider how you might find a way to use this resource.

I expect a return message soon.

Your Infernal Mentor,

Shacklebolt

Master Tempter, I.T.B.

My now studious young tempter, Pinegrub,

I see by your missive that you have done your homework. I am gladdened to know that you took my advice to heart. You correctly identified the young man's faith as Shiite Muslim. You also correctly identified the schism between the Sunni and the Shiite sects of the Muslim faith.

The new gang member (Amir) poses no danger to your charge. I say this only to confirm what you've already written. You were correct that the Muslim faith denies the deity of Jesus Christ. That alone is sufficient to render them a false faith. I know that I've told you this before, but I'll say it once again to drive the point home. Jesus, the Christ told his disciples, "I am the Way, the Truth, and the Life. No one comes to the Father but by me." This is recorded in the Gospel of John chapter 14, verse 6.

You already know that Jesus was not just a man or a prophet. You would have a hard time believing how many of the humans don't know this. They either don't want to know, or they twist it into something more comfortable for their own minds. There are those that attempt to pay homage to what they call "the accomplishments" of Jesus by acknowledging him as a prophet.

There are those yet that dig in their heels and say he was just a very charismatic man. A wonderful teacher, yes, but not a prophet and certainly not the son of God. There are some that try to interject that Jesus was a fictitious figure that never really existed. They say this even in the face of ancient historical documents that bear witness to his existence.

I recommend that you conduct a study of your own. Look at all the world's faiths. When I say all, I mean all. I will be asking you about the varying faiths as time goes on. I expect you to be able to give me an intelligent and coherent answer. I've read all the material printed on these faiths. I want your answers in your own words. Don't give me a verbatim answer from a book or scroll. If you can put it in your own words, then I know you understand it.

You already know most of the various versions of false Christianity. The first two that I want you to look at are Hinduism and Buddhism. These two faiths represent a huge percentage of the world's population. If you know their beliefs and tenets, you will be able to work from within them to keep their practitioners trapped.

Here is a small example supposing that the faith in question is Hinduism. A Hindu practitioner believes in reincarnation. Here is an old ploy you can use to lend credence to this belief. A demon can use his whisper to influence the dreams of their charge. In some instances, you can use your whisper to provide your charge a vision if they are in a meditative state.

Here is an example of how to use this. Let us suppose that your charge is on a search for the truth. As laughable as a human searching for the truth is, let us proceed with that notion. You could use your whisper to suggest that they investigate Hinduism. Hindu beliefs come from a completely different culture, so the beliefs are a bit alien to Western culture. That doesn't mean they aren't easily embraced by someone seeking to hide from the truth.

After your charge has done a fair bit of research into the Hindu faith, he will become familiar with the idea of reincarnation. One lives out their life in this body, and when they die, they move on to either reward or temporary punishment to be born again. That is a doctrine that is extremely attractive to humankind. Behind the idea of reincarnation is the thought of avoiding eternal punishment for acts done in this life.

If a person lives a particularly wicked life, their punishment in the next life could be that you return as a cockroach. Depending on the species, your life would be as short as one hundred days or up to two years. In the mind of some people, that is a small price to pay for doing whatever you want to do in the life you are living now. Reincarnation gives them the license to ignore morality without punishment.

In our scenario, your charge is now aware of reincarnation. He finds it attractive. Let's admit that it is a bit hard to swallow from the standpoint of Western culture. That is where you and your whisper come in. If your charge spends any time at all in meditation, you can send him visions of himself. The trick to it is that you send him visions of himself as he is now but in a setting in the far past.

Demon kind went a bit overboard on this one in the last century. Tempters weren't communicating with each other, and that caused a problem. How many people can claim they were George Washington in a past life? The two that really stood out were King Tut and Cleopatra. For a time, a month didn't go by without someone claiming they were one of these famous people in a past life.

That was too easy to refute. If the soul of Abraham Lincoln is now in the body of a plumber from Vermont, how could that same reincarnated soul also inhabit the bodies of seven other people across the U.S.? Credibility for this subject has been rebuilt over time. We have garnered a large following over the past twenty years.

The visions that you send your charge should show him in a favorable light. He is the fearless leader saving his men from disaster. He is the noble fighter defending the rights of the poor and downtrodden. He is the sole survivor of a hopeless battle for a noble cause.

This is the same tactic that a human con man would use. You play on their vanity, and they respond by wanting to believe. If you can instill the desire to believe, it will make your job much easier. Whisper to him that deep down, he still has this noble or fearless spirit. This sort of drivel always gets the attention of the weak-minded.

Your charge is extremely indoctrinated in the Catholic faith. You won't have to worry about trying to lead him into a false faith. You will need to study this skill for use in the future. This tactic takes on more of the deceiver aspect of your job, rather than just the tempter.

I expect your studies to be in-depth. In your next message, let me know the sources you use for your studies. You will not use magazines. I expect you to scour historical tomes. I want you to reference at least one ancient scroll.

In your next message, I want an update on Maria. Let me know how things are standing between her and your charge. How are they getting along? Is she still fixated on our young man? Does she have genuine feelings, or is she, as I suspect, just using him? Give me an update on Julian and one on Daniel. Keep me apprised of his relationship with his mother.

You didn't give me much information on Amir. If he is vocal about his faith, you can use him as a foil against your charge. They could get into some very lively (and possibly violent) debates about their faiths. You have your instructions.

Your Infernal Mentor,

Shacklebolt

Master Tempter, I.T.B.

My surprising young tempter, Pinegrub,

I was especially pleased with your news. Maria says she is pregnant and that the father is our Carlos. This is absolutely delicious. Your message described their conversation when she broke the news to him. I wish I could have witnessed that. The way you described his reaction was intriguing.

You indicated that he went through the standard shock, a moment of confusion, a moment of wonder, and finally settling on fear. I can understand why you say he shifted into suspicion not long after. He knew he wasn't her first. He wasn't even sure he was her only paramour now. That thought made him suspicious.

Your message indicated that she treated the news of her pregnancy as a problem. She didn't seem scared. It just seemed to be a situation that needed to be dealt with. You could have caused a real schism between them if you could have prompted her to tell him she'd done it before. I assume, from the tone of your message, that she has had a previous abortion.

Our self-righteous young Catholic is facing a dilemma. Moments like these reveal the commitment a person has to their faith. You stated that she asked him for the money to get an abortion. I'm sure your young man is struggling with that. He isn't committed to her but hates the idea of killing his child in the womb.

Your young charge is facing one of the biggest decisions of his life. How important are his beliefs? Does he really believe, or is it just a set of rules he was trained to by his parents? What he decides in this situation will show his true character. This is where you need to implement your whisper and your imps.

Whisper to him that he is too young to be a father. Imply that he hasn't the first clue about being a parent. Tell him he isn't ready. Call out to him that he has no way of knowing that the baby is really his. If you can prompt him to confront Maria with this thought, it will cause even more distress.

Give him some time to stew in his moral struggle. After you've planted those seeds, merely repeat them. In a few days, he will begin to even out. That will tell you that he is grappling with the problem and getting close to deciding. This is where you push him to make the decision you want.

Give him what he will think is a way out morally. Tell him if she has an abortion that is on her. She will be the one making the choice, not him. He can't be held responsible for the things that she does, can he? He would only be giving her money. What she does with it would be her business.

This is a way for him to moralize his part in it. He is only a bystander. He won't see himself as an expectant father condoning the death of his future child. The best part for us is this. That is exactly what he will be, and deep down, he knows it. It will take him time to admit it to himself, but it will be too late by then. He will have played a part in the death of his unborn baby.

That fact alone will give you ample ammunition in the future. If he ever leans toward the cross, just remind him of his moral failure when a life was at stake. Tell him it is the same thing as watching a loved one being run over by a car when he could have done something about it. Isn't that the same as wanting someone you love to die?

Then remind him of his failed faith. Tell him he is a phony. Tell him that any good thoughts he has of himself are a lie, and he knows it. Remind him of how ashamed of him his mother would be. That line of thought gives you more leverage over him.

Have Maria's tempter whisper that she can control Carlos with this information. All she must do is threaten to tell his mother that he gave her the money to abort their precious baby. She was confused and scared. She didn't know what to do and went to Carlos for advice. He was the one who brought up abortion, not her.

This is a tactic that you will use after their relationship is ended. I can tell you from his background that this decision, one way or another, is going to end it. If they go forward with the abortion; and they probably will, he will see her as an object of loathing because she exposed how low he really is.

If he fights her on the abortion, it will become common knowledge that he slept around. Most people wouldn't think of that as a big deal. To him, however, it would disappoint and hurt his mother. We both know she would get over that. She would accept and love the child as her grandchild. Carlos, however, will not be thinking along those lines.

You have that young man right where you want him. He is in a terribly uncomfortable state. He will remain in that state because he doesn't see a way through it. He doesn't want a child because he isn't ready to be a father. He doesn't want a child because he knows he can't afford a child. He doesn't want a child out of wedlock because he knows it will disappoint his mother. He doesn't want a reputation just like the reputations of so many other young Hispanic men.

He has his Catholic beliefs, but they will matter little in the face of all of this. He will hand over the money and curse Maria in his heart. As far as he is concerned, it is all her fault. If she didn't want to get pregnant, she should have taken precautions.

This will all lead him down the path of his own victimhood. If he doesn't have to face his responsibility, he won't. That is human nature. He won't admit his wrong until he is made to.

I've used a great deal of this message to address the situation you are cultivating. The expenditure is worth it. You couldn't have hoped for a better situation to distract and drag down your charge. You will be able to keep him preoccupied with this for years.

Let us suppose for a moment that Maria doesn't get the abortion. She will have a hold over Carlos' life for at least the next eighteen years. He will have to pay for the child's upkeep. He will have to try to get along with her for the sake of his child. At his age, the next eighteen years working with and answering to her will seem like torture. He won't want to do that in the least.

I can promise you that these thoughts will occur to him. They will because you will whisper them to him. By the time you are finished whispering to him, lining out a horrible future, he will gladly hand over the money and meekly ask her to have the abortion. In the current society, you can't lose this one.

Keep me informed of your progress in this. Keep an eye on Maria and let me know what she is doing behind your charge's back. I want an update concerning Julian. Does he know of the pregnancy? Does anyone else suspect? We could possibly use this to cause a schism between Julian and Carlos.

Your task has been made much easier providing you remain diligent. No falling asleep on watch, or you will regret it.

Your Infernal Mentor,

Shacklebolt

Master Tempter, I.T.B.

My wily young tempter, Pinegrub,

I could hardly believe my eyes when I read your message. You are having a wonderful streak of luck. You are experiencing, in your third time out as a tempter, what other tempters would give their fangs to experience. Where to begin?

By your descriptions up to this point, Carlos is a stubborn young man who will only do things his way. You said he seemed to be working through the idea of Maria aborting their child. Then you provide me with the shock that Maria is attempting to blackmail Carlos with it. She wants the money to pay for the abortion and an additional two thousand dollars. Otherwise, she will go to his mother.

That alone, understandably threw your young charge completely off balance. I'm sure he didn't conceive of this happening at all. He is going through a combination of rage and fear that has him utterly flummoxed. In this situation, you have him completely at your mercy.

This situation in his mind is bad enough. Then your charge finds out that his younger brother has expressed interest in the gang. That is understandable. The younger brother sees his older brother as worldly and, as they say, "cool." This makes him want to emulate his older sibling.

At the age of fourteen, the gang leader Julian is taking a serious look at young Andre. The child still has the appearance of innocence. That is a valuable tool in the hands of a group leader, especially one bent on less than innocent employment. The adolescent will make a good lookout, or better yet, an ignorant courier.

You say that Carlos has heard of his brother's interest, but he doesn't know of Julian's interest in him. That will add fuel to the fire that is currently consuming your charge's attention. This may well push him past one of his breaking points. We will have to watch this and see.

You realize that he will worry that his brother will find out about the pregnancy. Then a whole host of issues will crop up in his mind. Will his brother go to their mother with the information? Will he try to blackmail Carlos in the same way that Maria is attempting? Your charge will develop severe trust issues because of this. You simply must smile about it.

Your job with Carlos is made so easy by the circumstances. This is where you plan ahead. His brother will be open to your influence soon. The young man still hasn't reached his age of accountability. His age is sufficient, but his mother has sheltered him. He is ignorant of the ways of his fellow fallen humans. His older brother doesn't know how innocent Andre remains.

Consider, though, he is still protected. Don't get ahead of yourself and start trying to directly tempt the child. That will bring a charge of angels right at you. You could, however, send a young girl close to his age to test his metal. You can't tempt him directly, but you can use another human to tempt him.

From your description of the gang, there are several young ladies you could use for this. They are all lower in the pecking order than Maria. She would be aware of the activities of the other girls. Without her approval, none of the girls would make a move. If you are considering this venue, I would suggest Alicia. Of the girls, she is the most obedient to Maria.

I notice that you haven't sent me any information on Julian, Daniel, or Amir. You need to keep up with what is going on with them. There is too much potential there for you to let it go to waste. Have Carlos and Amir had any disagreements about their faiths? If they have not, a good way for you to prompt one is to suggest to Carlos that he should cross himself before a meal with the gang.

The Muslim gang member will find that rather upsetting. You could suggest your charge to bring some of his mother's homemade pork cracklings to the gang. The gang would love them, and they would be particularly upsetting to Amir. He would see it as antagonism from your charge. It would be something to exclude him from the group.

These are just a couple of things you could do to foment trouble between the two. Use your imagination and see what you can come up with. You won't be exercising your creativity if I am the one providing the scenarios you use.

Consider that when you incite your charge to antagonize Amir because of faith, you are helping damage the reputation of Christianity. The world at large considers Catholicism a Christian faith. It aids our cause when we can make Christians appear unloving and intolerant.

You either forgot or left out information on Julian in your report. Aside from his interest in Andre as a possible gang member, there was nothing. I want to know if he knows about the pregnancy. It seems to me that would be a major issue. Julian is already suspicious of Carlos. This would be the proverbial straw that broke the camel's back. If he isn't aware, is it because she is keeping it from him or, is her pregnancy a lie? That would be a good way for Maria to extort money from him.

You mentioned in your report that Carlos has been brought up on charges of assault and battery. Your report explained that the mother of a younger teen filed the charges. In an enraged state, your charge accused another younger boy of "disrespecting" him and soundly beat him. You used your imps to drive your charge into a higher frenzy by inferring that he was weak.

I must warn you against that in the future. Your charge is safely under your influence. You don't want to push him into doing something that he will soon regret. That will cause him to question the path he has taken. You never want your charge to do that. It is dangerous to our cause.

When a human questions the actions that brought them to an undesirable situation, they look at their motivations. From there, it is a short jump to examining their philosophy and beliefs. Those are the moments that the Creator looks for. Moments such as these are when the lost typically reach out to him.

That is when He "conveniently" sends in one of His redeemed. The saved individual comes along with answers to questions. Unlike what most humans believe, conversion is very seldom a sudden thing. It usually takes the seeds of salvation to be sown multiple times for the lost soul to respond. Doubt and fear are powerful weapons.

It is our grip on society that aids us here. The herd mentality and human nature make it very unfashionable to bear witness to the gospel of Christ. It is fear of being unacceptable to those around them that keeps many from responding. The Creator made humankind to be social beings. That is one of the things that works in our favor.

Keep me apprised of the legal situation your charge has placed himself in. I don't like that you allowed him to be pushed into stepping out of his normal character. This could be the beginning of an opening for the enemy that we don't want.

I also want a report on the activity of Daniel. I realize he isn't your charge, but he is in the orbit of your charge. When I tell you I want something, you go get it. You do not question me, and you don't demand justification for the order.

It appears you may be slipping back into behavior that you should be guarding against. I don't mind a question here and there. You won't learn if you don't ask. However, an imperious attitude is something you will not take with me. If I see that flow across a message again, you will regret it. I believe your instructions are clear enough.

Your Infernal Mentor,

Shacklebolt

Master Tempter, I.T.B.

My sufficiently humble tempter, Pinegrub,

I received your message and found aspects of it rather curious. After I got through all the groveling and apologizing for your attitude, I found several nuggets of interest. You have a suspicion that Maria isn't pregnant. You base this on a conversation you heard between two of the girls.

It appears that Maria has done this not once but twice before. She watches for a young man who appears to be a go-getter in the gang. She tempts the prospective source of cash, sleeps with them several times, and then springs the trap.

I hope you understand that on this issue, we can't be satisfied with uncertainty. You need to find out if she is pregnant or not. Some of the more delicate plans we have for the future depend on it. There is no sense in making plans based on a nebulous if.

Has your charge heard any of these rumors? This could prove to be the thing that will push him from the gang. In case you are wondering, we don't want that. We've had this young man eating from your palm since he joined the gang. Haven't you noticed that he listens to your whisper with much more ease now?

I have to keep reminding myself of your inexperience with humanity. Any other tempter would have investigated these facts without prompting. If it turned out that she is pregnant, there would be no need to even bring it up. Instead, I guide you through the simple process of tracking down the information you should already have.

Task two of your imps to keep track of Maria. Instruct them to listen to every word she says. They should take note of who she talks to in person or on her cell phone. Explain to them that they are looking for evidence of her pregnancy. She is bound to have a doctor's report or some evidence if it is true. I want that piece of information before we go forward with anything else concerning her.

Your information about Julian was surprising. You stated that he is considering expanding his territory. He seems to want to include a four-block area that is currently the territory of a Hispanic gang. The only way a gang gains territory is through violence. Investigate this and report back to me. I want to know if Julian is entertaining the idea or making plans to get what he wants.

You did confirm the trouble between Amir and Carlos. I was

amused at the "almost fight" you say they had. Your description of them as two angry puppies was especially funny. You have confirmed that neither can tolerate the openly practiced faith of the other. We will have to see how Julian handles this discrepancy.

I was just a bit disappointed in the tactic you used to cause the problem between your charge and Amir. You don't have to do everything exactly as I describe it. I told you to use your imagination. Those weren't idle words. I want you to try to develop your own style. You won't grow adept at tempting and seducing a human soul unless you try to do it on your own.

You have, however, succeeded in stirring up antagonism between the two. That means that you are making progress in the direction you want to go. I expect you to continue this. For now, I want you to use small barbs to keep the contempt alive between them. We can't amp up the conflict until we know what direction Julian will go on this issue. I'm not going to tell you how to do this. I want you to at least try to be creative.

Your report on Daniel was equally surprising. You said that Daniel has two friends that are highly placed in a Hispanic gang. This is the very same gang that Julian is considering challenging for territory. This is an interesting development. You need to find out all that you can about young Daniel's activities.

Were these friends of a long acquaintance or newly made friends? Why is he keeping company with members of a rival gang? I am assuming that the young man is aware of their placement in the gang. After you describe him as cunning and intelligent, I would not anticipate him to be so uninformed.

I realize that you only have so many imps to do the work. I am assigning you three more imps temporarily for this research. I want to know what is going on between these gangs. It sounds as though something might be going on that we need to know about. When the imps report to you, assign them to watch over Daniel and the two gang members.

I see that you were able to mitigate your charge's legal situation. You are finally starting to make connections and form your own network. That is how we get things done. I'm sure you had to do some trading of favors to get it done, but that is your business. The more you can get completed on your own, the more capable you look to those above you. You may consider yourself taking a step toward autonomy.

You were not able to get the case dismissed against him. That is disappointing at your level but not unexpected. While we have a good deal of influence over the justice system, our control is not absolute. There is human free will to be considered in dealing with humans. That is one of our stumbling blocks.

I will tell you that tempting humans to gross sin has become much easier over this last generation. The influence of the Holy Spirit is on the wane. If you look around, you will see things speeding up. I am assuming that you've done your reading of the Bible as I recommended some time back.

What I am saying here is that humanity is in a state of greater rebellion against the Creator. If you've studied the book of Daniel and the book of Revelation as you were instructed when you accepted your position as a tempter, you would know we are on the brink of change. We don't know exactly what the change is or even when it will occur, but we know it is coming.

Let's get back to business. Your charge has to endure one counseling session per week for the next twenty-six weeks. That is a comparatively light sentence for such a violent crime. We have the legal system looking at it as a first offense. The violence of the act nor the mindset of the offender is considered, in most cases.

The degree of control we have assumed over human society is impressive. Common sense is being largely ignored. We have the legal system more concerned with the rights of the accused rather than the victim's rights. A woman who has been violently raped and beaten will be asked if she intentionally tempted the men who committed the crime. What they've allowed us to do is hilarious.

I found your description of the counselor assigned to Carlos rather odd. You wrote that you couldn't get a feel for their intent. You stated that when you paid attention to them, it was almost like they weren't there. I have seen this several times before. There is something about their makeup that makes them unreadable.

You will need to watch them during their sessions before you can judge intent. When I say watch them, I mean it. Pay attention to what is said and how Carlos reacts to it. Some humans are good at passing meaning inside of a seemingly empty statement. "How have you been doing lately?" seems like an innocent question. It is a biting reprisal coming from a disillusioned friend to a recently recovering alcoholic. In situations like this, you are looking for nuance in a conversation.

You have your instructions, and I have other duties to attend. It seems my records are being audited by his lordship Insidious Dream. I suspect this is at the prompting of that little twit Argass. He is probably trying to impress his lordship at my expense. What he doesn't know is that I've been at this far longer than he has.

Your Infernal Mentor,

Shacklebolt

Master Tempter, I.T.B.

My slowly learning tempter, Pinegrub,

I am gratified that every time I emphasize the gravity of a situation, you react appropriately. After your first charge, I began to think you were a hopeless case that I would have to dispose of. You have since, for the most part, redeemed your usefulness to our cause.

You found out that Maria is pregnant. I found it greatly amusing that she really was trying to set a trap for Carlos but forgot to take precautions. The very thing she was going to use against him became a reality.

Is the rumor that she's had a previous abortion true? Is she suffering any emotional distress at the thought of disposing of this baby? I ask because I've seen many women who have had previous abortions that have a hard time living with it. When another unwanted pregnancy occurs, they usually have the baby and give it up for adoption. A good percentage of the distressed who proceed with the second abortion commit suicide not long afterward (with our prompting, of course).

From our perspective, it is like being invited into a candy store with an unlimited budget. They are already so guilt-ridden that anything goes. They realize they've ended the lives of two babies. Most of them don't feel they deserve to live. Those are prime hunting grounds for us. We must do our worst before they reach out to the Creator for forgiveness.

You say that Carlos has heard the rumors of her past deceptions and confronted her with them. He had nothing to offer in response when she showed him the positive results from the doctor's reports. Your report indicated that he considered pressing for a paternity test. He seemed to have thought better of it when he considered her reaction. He didn't want her to raise the blackmail amount and then run to his mother for spite.

Do you have any idea how he plans to raise the money? Has he been able to save any money, or has he been giving all of it to his mother? I was under the impression that she wouldn't accept cash from him because of her fear of what he was doing to get it

Has anything changed in that respect? Does his mother accept money from him now? Does she have any idea where his money comes from? I'm sure she has some vague idea that it isn't honest money. Is his income stream steady, or does it depend on the errands that he takes care of for Julian?

The information you uncovered about Daniel and his two friends was almost startling. He is awfully young to have such ambitious and far-reaching plans. So, young Daniel wants to be a lieutenant under one of his friends. That is interesting. It shows some forethought.

Most young men want to be the leader without giving thought to all that entails. Our young traitor has been studying the leader, his responsibilities, and his liabilities by your description. By his estimation, leadership isn't worth all the work to maintain it. He has decided that middle management is the perfect place for him.

Your self-important three-man team has decided not only to topple the leadership in the Hispanic gang, but they also plan to take over this one when that job is done. While their plans are rather well thought out, there are too many factors that can go wrong.

I predict that they will be unsuccessful. Their lack of success will probably get all three killed. One, possibly two, of them are being driven by demonic whisper to reach for this prize. They are relying solely on cunning and timing. That isn't enough.

Don't do anything with this situation. We can use the power grab to our advantage. The best-case scenario would be to have Carlos elevated in the gang hierarchy. We practically own his soul already. We might as well seal the deal by putting him in a position where he feels obligated to lead.

Your report indicates that we've lost the prospect of Andre joining the gang. You say you were surprised when Carlos went to his mother with the news instead of confronting Julian. It sounds like your charge reasoned this out before acting. The mother would have a much stronger hold over Andre at his age.

Your report didn't contain much detail in this area. Were you able to sow some discord in the family while the problem was addressed? You could have influenced your charge's attitude toward the gang concerning his younger brother. That would have opened the door to their mother, asking how it was alright for him then.

That would have the effect of turning Carlos' argument around on himself. The mother would have the grounds to start beating the dead horse of getting Carlos out of the gang. That, in turn, would have raised the resentment level between the two all over again. Remember that she loves her son and doesn't want him doing wrong.

Instruct the imp that you have at their mother's house to start shouting things to her. "You are losing your children to the gang!" and "The gang is going to tear your family apart!" Ensure that this litany is repeated over and over for days.

This will have the wonderful effect of making her extremely hostile toward the subject of the gang. She will see her family as being in danger just by their presence in the neighborhood. This will put us in a good position to push her in one of two directions.

She has been pushing Carlos to leave the gang. If we start using our resources to tear down her support system, she will do one of two things. Her choices will be to bend her principles and accept help from Carlos or move her family to another neighborhood.

Your messages so far indicate that she is a cleaning lady for two separate upscale families. Her family depends on that income to survive. They receive food stamps, but that assistance is never enough. It would be a simple matter for you to make it appear as though she has stolen something of value from one or both families.

Once she has lost one or both families as clients, she will unlikely find other clients in time to help. She will be left with the immediate choice to accept help from Carlos or let her children go without. She is a proud woman but, concern for her children's well-being will overcome her pride.

I want you to ride around on Carlo's shoulder for the foreseeable future. You will need to take a direct hand in influencing him. Chatter at him about how his mother is so unbending. I'm sure he is still smarting after their meeting about Andre's future. If he sees her as unbending, it will have the effect of making him just as rigid.

Don't worry about the mother's future troubles. I will take care of that part. Just be ready for action. By the time his mother approaches Carlos with her worries, she will be sufficiently humbled.

Seeing his mother in this position will enrage him. He will be furious that anyone would accuse his mother of stealing. He will be angry that God allowed this to happen to such a gentle soul. Meantime, she will be asking this very same question. He will become resigned in his lack of faith, and she will be questioning hers.

Remember to send me information on Carlos' financial situation. I want more information on Daniel and his two cronies.

Find out about Maria's history with abortion. See if you can find out more about Julian's plans for the other gang. You may keep the three imps I loaned you for now. I realize that I have given you many irons in the fire. This is how we cover our bases.

Your Infernal Mentor,

Shacklebolt

Master Tempter, I.T.B.

My finally attentive tempter, Pinegrub,

I see by your message that this is Maria's first pregnancy. She did what a lot of con men do after running a successful con over and over. She got too confident and ignored the little details. Now she is faced with the reality of a child she didn't plan for and doesn't want.

You have an excellent opportunity here to wring some torture out of a human that isn't your charge. I know you can't tempt her directly. She has a tempter already, and that would be bad form on your part. What you can do is make suggestions.

You are obviously on speaking terms with her tempter. Ask him if she has shown any secret desire to have a baby at some far-off time in the future. If he doesn't know, continue the line of thought by asking if she dotes on her younger siblings. If she doesn't have siblings, then ask about nieces and nephews.

Her tempter is in a position to cause her great emotional pain. She has figuratively aborted children before. Suggest that he can whisper to her that it was her wish all along. Tell her she is an uncaring, selfish woman.

What is her relationship with her mother? Are they on speaking terms? If they are, what are her mother's views on the subject? Has she had an abortion? Would she react as strongly as Carlos' mother?

Here is a wonderful way for you to kick the beehive, as they say. You informed me that Maria had a doctor's report she showed Carlos. If Maria lives with her mother, what would her mother do if a letter from the Doctor's office came in the mail for Maria? Would she open it out of concern for her daughter?

That would get the ball rolling nicely. Maria would have to defend herself from her mother's wrath. That would introduce a new element into the equation. The more we upset her, the more she will transfer over to Carlos. She will tell herself that this is all his fault.

In this aspect of the situation, we will need to explore scenarios. Which one will yield us the most pain and sorrow? You were there the night Maria tempted Carlos into her bed. You didn't know her tempter had occupied her mind with the sole purpose of making her forget to take precautions against this outcome.

After Maria's mother is brought into the mix, it will be a

simple matter to include Carlos' mother. What we must decide is what do we want out of this. We could use this pregnancy to wreak havoc in the lives of all those concerned. That would include the life of an innocent baby.

Nothing draws financial resources like the birth and upkeep of a baby. We could have them so torn by their own unfulfilled wants and desires. That is not even considering the guilt we could riddle them with when they secretly wish the baby didn't exist. A worn and weary young parent is easily led into that train of thought when money is always short, and there is no light at the end of the tunnel.

You wouldn't even have to whisper it outright to them. A well-thought-out innuendo is enough. Say something like, "Remember how much fun Friday nights were before the baby?" That is along the same lines as this one. "When was the last time you got to go out with your friends?"

The current moral state of society has degraded nicely because of our efforts. The thought of giving up a child or handing a child over to the state was unspeakable a generation ago. That is one of the good things about our longevity. We see things change over time that the humans don't see. Their lifetimes are so short that they are unaware of the degree of change that happens over a generation.

I need more information on Maria's state of mind and her relationship with her mother. Does Julian have any idea about her pregnancy? That could be a potential monkey wrench we could throw into the works. If we were to encourage Julian to believe that Carlos has no intention of living up to his responsibilities, that would be interesting.

At this point, we know that the pregnancy is real. We also have a good plan on what we can do if the child is brought into the world. We also have a good avenue of attack if the child is aborted. Since we have such a wide variety of possibilities, we should run this past our chain of command.

I'm quite sure I know what his lordship will tell us to do. He will instruct us to seek the death of the baby. Abortion is anathema to the Creator. To him, all life is precious, even the lives of the disadvantaged. Our lordship will see this as a way of casting an insult into the face of the Creator.

I know you will be disappointed. You must consider the humans are our hated enemies. They are loved by the Creator as His children. The more innocents we can remove from the game, the fewer will surface as Christians and ruin our plans later. I will, however, abide by the decision made by his lordship.

Your report indicates that Daniel and his two friends are doing nothing more than an ambitious power play. It is no threat to our plans. We can even use them to forward our goals. Who knows what kind of mayhem we can push them to?

I see that Carlos' mother is devastated by her loss of position with both families. It was a simple matter to handle. The youngest child of one of the families is prone to theft. That same child has a real problem owning his flaws.

I arranged an exposure of his theft to one of his victims. By the time the offended party confronted him, the situation was volatile. The young man had proof of the thief's guilt and threatened to use it. Our thief promised his victim a large sum of cash in return for his silence.

From there, it was a simple matter for the young thief to steal several items of value from his mother's jewelry cabinet. When the theft was noticed, he nonchalantly mentioned that Rosa was the last person he saw go into the master bedroom. He never outright accused her of theft. He just let his parents draw their own conclusions.

Rosa was summarily accused, and a warrant was obtained. The jewelry was never found, and the police detective stated that he believed her innocence. When he asked who had offered up the accusation against Mrs. Rodriguez, the detective was told of their son's recollection. He called the motive into question and was summarily dismissed.

The family was unwilling to continue any investigation at all. They released Mrs. Rodriguez from their service and contacted the other client family. They were (on some level) aware of her innocence. They were, however, unable to accept that their child could sink so low as to steal from his mother and cost a trusted servant their livelihood.

I can promise you that if she isn't sufficiently humbled at this time, we have other situations we can engineer. We must walk a fine line, though. Rosa is a Catholic. That means she believes in God. We can't push her so far that she reaches out to the Creator for help. He would send her someone to guide her into salvation. We need to keep her downtrodden but not desperate.

Keep your imps shouting at her. Tell her how she isn't providing for her family. Urge her to accept help from Carlos. That is why he joined the gang in the first place. Your primary weapon on her from this point on is guilt. Do what you can to make her feel like a failure. Soon, she will feel forlorn enough that she will begin to bend.

See if you can get me more information on Daniel's associates. We may be able to cause a great deal of trouble within both gangs. We know almost nothing now. Find out what you can and report back to me.

I am still waiting for the financial information for your charge. If you don't send me the information I've asked for in your next message, you will be heartily punished. I don't ask for things to marvel at my own planning ability. I need that information. You have sufficient instruction. Now get to work.

Your Infernal Mentor,

Shacklebolt
Master Tempter, I.T.B.

My busy tempter, Pinegrub,

My, my, my, haven't you been busy. I opened this message to a wealth of information. That last threat must have put the fear of me into you. I suspect you remember your previous punishment and sincerely didn't want to lose another body part. That is a good choice on your part. Your parts grow back, but they itch monstrously while they do.

I see that Carlos has saved a good deal of money. Giving Maria the money to kill their baby and buy her silence won't be a problem. He will have to worry about her future silence, though. I don't think I need to tell you to plant that seed and keep it well watered. This brings me to the decision I would acquire for you.

I spoke personally with his lordship. Regarding allowing the child to live or to have it aborted, he took only moments to decide. If it is within our power to influence the baby's death, that is what we must do. They are our enemy. We are to seek the death and destruction of all the unborn we can. Their deaths grieve the Creator.

His lordship informed me that we are to provide the time and location of the abortion should it happen. Our division is being paid a visit from the demon prince Molech. You should know that he dedicated himself to child sacrifice in ancient times.

In this city, we have two doctors performing abortions that are devotees of Molech. His lordship would like to be able to present a ceremony of sacrifice through the abortion to Molech. It would go a long way to engendering goodwill between our division and this powerful demon prince.

You will keep me informed about this situation with any new developments. I want to be able to keep his lordship abreast of the situation. He has five other potential abortions in the works. For some reason, he has decided that he wants to use this one if possible. I think it is because both parents believe in God. This will show them how traitorous they are to their own beliefs.

As I understand it, his lordship plans for Maria to awaken early from the anesthesia. When a baby is aborted, one of the personnel assembles the pieces. This is done to ensure that none of the developing baby is left inside the mother. His lordship plans for her eyes to fall her upon her reassembled baby just as they dispose of it. A veritable cloud of imps screaming condemnation will descend upon her.

His exact words were, "That will be a nice offering of life and despair for the demon prince. He will be well pleased." This is something done to show allegiance and respect of much greater power. The act will curry much favor from Molech. You can rest assured that his lordship InsidiousDream is looking to climb the ladder of the demonic chain of command.

I see that you were able to cause some trouble for Daniel and his associates. In your message, you stated that you merely exposed their plans. You said nothing of how the gang leader reacted to such a plot going on behind his back. I would be most interested to hear of it. Perhaps there is a situation we can use to our advantage.

Finally! You give me good news concerning your charge's mother. It would seem, a taste of failure has humbled her a bit. She has deigned to accept help from her oldest son. I promise you; this is a bitter pill for her to swallow. You should savor every moment this woman tastes defeat. This is a valuable tool to widen the gap between herself and her son.

You must understand that we can't divert our attention away from Carlos. We must keep our efforts concentrated on him. He is your charge, not her. Her pain and discomfort are simply an added bonus for you. Have you kept your imps chewing away at his sense of self-worth? Do not let up on that young man.

Don't mistake me. I don't want you to stay away from the mother. I just want to make sure you don't push her too far. It is as I warned you before. The woman has a real reverence for God. I hope you understand that the Creator knows of this reverence. To his mind, she is simply misled.

This is the sort of situation the He will let us wear her down. Then, when she is at her wit's end, He would send in one of his saints to show her love and compassion. That would be our undoing. Once she recognized that a true Christian wasn't her enemy, it would be the beginning of the end for us in her life.

All of His effective witnesses approach the lost from a perspective of love and concern. I will grant you that we have our hands stirring the pot enough to make the dish all but inedible. You need to understand, that love and compassion are the keys to sharing the Gospel of Christ.

As far as interpersonal contact goes, that is what we guard against. We have the obnoxious passerby say something snide or cruel. Something that small is enough to remind the lost of their lives and the upset that listening to this "strange" gospel will cause them.

When a simple remark isn't enough, we have one or more of our lost souls interrupt the conversation. We occasionally must resort to more disruptive methods. That includes violence if needed. We have to be careful in these instances, though. Remember that the great commission was the last commandment of the Redeemer. He protects the opportunities that He brings about.

When I say He protects those opportunities, I mean it. I can tell you from personal experience that the heavenly host is just waiting to attack. I've been in two such skirmishes. I was a young tempter when the first one happened.

My mentor had directed me to guard my charge and let no one near him with the Gospel. As a young demon, I took that order very seriously. All my imps were on this young man when one of his cousins approached him out of concern for his soul.

I put myself between them while my imps formed a circle around the man. Before I could register what was happening, a company of angels crashed into our midst like a bomb going off. I was thrown fifty yards, lost an arm and a leg. Two of my imps were banished immediately. The last three fled smoking from the area. I believe one was still burning from the holy light.

I tell you this so that you can understand that while he is yours to tempt. You don't have total sway over him. There are things you can't do, and there are things you won't be allowed to do. Always keep in the back of your mind that humans are granted free will. Free will is nothing if they aren't given the opportunity to exercise it. You need to watch your boundaries in that sense. To do less is to risk your existence in this dimension.

I need information on Julian and his plans. Does he know anything more about Daniel and his friends? What is the timeframe of his plans to make a move on the other gang?

Your Infernal Mentor,

Shacklebolt

Master Tempter, I.T.B.

My diligent tempter, Pinegrub,

You say your imps have informed you, Daniel and his friends are in trouble with the leader of "Los Jefes." That is such an amusing statement. It speaks to the arrogance and pride of man on a fundamental level. They aren't the bosses of much of anything. They don't realize they are constantly manipulated by us.

Your report in this area was lacking. I realize you are giving me the information as it was given to you. That is the problem. You need to learn how to get more detailed information from your imps. Since this is the first leadership position you've been in, you probably use a non-threatening leadership style. That is a mistake.

Your imps answer to you in the same way that you answer to me. You control a good deal of their fate. You may not be able to administer much in the way of punishment, but a word from you gets them the punishment they deserve. Consider that you wield authority over them. That authority includes punishment. You need to start using that branch of your power. It will gain you superior results.

You indicated in your report that Carlos has been going to his counseling sessions for a month now. You say you still can't seem to get a read on his counselor. That is rather unusual. Have you been sitting in on his counseling sessions? If not, you need to from this point on. Those sessions will provide insight into how your charge's mind works.

I bring this up because this is the first time you mentioned the counselor since you first told me about him. After all this time, you should know something about the counselor. You should be able to tell me what kind of person he is. You should know something about his beliefs and practices because that will come out in his counseling style. I should not be hearing that you still can't get a read on him.

I hope you have reached the point that you are willing to work honestly with me. Unlike our strategy with humans, we can't work effectively together if we aren't honest. We deceive humans with lies. We tempt them to lie to each other. We perpetuate lies in their society. We do not lie to each other.

In your next message, I want as much information about the counselor as you can provide. I want details. You will give me exact information on his next counseling session. I want to know how your charge reacts to the counselor. Does the counselor try to gently draw the truth from your charge? Does he state facts coldly and then simply ask questions? Get me that information.

I see that Maria has made her appointment to have her abortion. You said that you had your imps screeching at her that she didn't want to be a parent. I see why her tempter accepted your help so readily. It made his job so much easier.

He was whispering to her that she wasn't ready. He was also reminding her of how much responsibility a newborn baby can be. From your report and the description of her tempter's strategy, I'm surprised she didn't attempt the abortion with a coat hanger.

The decision has been made. Now all of you need to back off her. Give her a chance to rationalize her sin to herself. Once she is comfortable enough with it, just tell her she is making the right choice. We don't want her to find her conscience and back out of it. That would embarrass our lordship.

Your message stated that Carlos has gathered the money to give to Maria. Don't let an opportunity pass. Make sure you constantly remind him that he is paying for her mistake. Tell him she should have taken precautions. They wouldn't be in this mess had it not been for her. She is the one who tempted him anyway.

If you keep up that dialog in the young man's ear, he will hand over the money in a very begrudging fashion. That is exactly what you want. You don't want Maria to view him as someone to come to when her guilt flares up. We want to make sure they both feel like victims. We don't want her talking to him without blame. We also want him to continually blame her.

We keep them continually blaming the other. They won't have the presence of mind to face what they're doing until a life is snuffed out. They should both face up to the new life they are responsible for, but they won't. If Maria's tempter does his job correctly, she will never face her part in this. If she does, she will be so misinformed, she will react in a self-destructive manner. We can only hope.

I am disturbed about your news of the mother. How did Ms. Rodriguez find a client so soon? I had gone to a good bit of trouble to ruin her employment. I know I had sabotaged her reputation in the social circles her former employers occupied.

This goes back to obtaining more accurate information from your imps. Something is going on that we are not aware of. By all the information you gave me, that woman should be a ragged mess of worry. I don't like this. Take at least one day to shadow her yourself. Don't trust what your imps are saying. Find out information on her for yourself. I want a detailed report of what she is doing.

I don't mean to worry you, but this could portend something larger going on in the background. Unexplained things happening like this is exactly the sort of thing that warns of the Heavenly Host being nearby. We need to ensure that our charge is safely on his path to destruction.

To do that, we need to foster an environment of doubt, disbelief, and discontent. We want these people looking to their own means to make things better. The last thing we want is for even one of them to kneel in sincere prayer. The instant one of these stupid monkeys realizes how close they are to the kingdom of Heaven, we are lost. Never forget, the Creator is never more than a sincere prayer away.

I say that in all sincerity. They don't realize that real forgiveness is theirs for the asking. It doesn't matter how far we've dragged them away from the light. They remain only a single step from their Heavenly Father. He will forgive them anything if only they will acknowledge it and sincerely turn from it.

I seem to have run off at a rant. Sorry about that. Sometimes I get so bothered because what is theirs for the asking is eternally denied to us. In my time doing this job, I've seen horrible sinners turn to the light. Murderers, rapists, child molesters, among the humans, forgiveness is for all who will repent and believe.

Something is off in everything that you have reported. I don't like the lack of information on the counselor. That, coupled with the mother finding employment so soon, is worrisome. Something is on the gameboard that we aren't seeing. Find it! I also want to know what is going on with Andre. If he is to be your future charge, don't you think you should be keeping up with him?

Get me the information that I require. Don't worry, we are the ones in charge here.

Your Infernal Mentor,

Shacklebolt

Master Tempter, I.T.B.

My very obedient tempter, Pinegrub,

I am so pleased with your performance. I did not expect you to have an honor guard of imps at the ready when myself, his lordship, and prince Molech arrived at the abortion clinic. I can tell you his lordship and the prince were very pleasantly surprised by your show of devotion and obeisance. I had not thought you'd have had the wherewithal to organize such a reception.

I suspect that you now owe not a few favors for such a display. I can tell you that you have found yourself in a very favorable light with his lordship. Prince Molech found the procession of imps with Maria to be especially pleasing. He especially liked the way two of them clung to her and whispered while one crawled up and down her body, screaming her worthlessness.

I had assigned you a single detachment of imps. What exactly did you trade in bargain for the other seven that I saw present? If you don't want to tell me, you don't have to. That was your business, after all. I just hope you haven't overextended yourself.

I apologize that you weren't allowed in the operating room. After all that work, I felt you deserved to be there. However, his lordship wanted it to be as intimate a setting for Prince Molech. It was an exquisite moment. You would have sincerely enjoyed it.

The doctor entered the room with no more emotion than a man tying his shoes. I will bet you almost anything that none of his peers know he is a worshipper of Molech. He substituted the tray used to hold the fetal remains with an identical tray made of solid silver.

The doctor believes that an offering of life should be treated with reverence. That is the reason for the silver tray. The nurse was unaware that his humming is a chant to Molech. His chant reached a crescendo as the baby was torn apart. She reassembled the baby after the abortion was completed.

Prince Molech was surprised when his lordship reached out and waved his hand over Maria, waking her. Her head was positioned perfectly when her eyes opened and came into focus. She saw the dismembered body of her baby. That was when the imps clinging to her started screaming her guilt at her.

To say the least, she became hysterical. The nurse hurriedly covered the tray. The doctor very calmly added a strong sedative to her

IV. The last thing she will remember is seeing the tray containing the bloody remains of her baby. The nurse had an orderly wheel her into the recovery room.

Prince Molech enjoyed the spike of despair and self-loathing that filled the room when Maria saw her baby. I swear to you, he seemed almost to be aroused at that moment. We, as demons, enjoy their torment. We even take enjoyment from their demise. He, on the other hand, seemed to take personal ecstasy. I would be lying to you if I told you he doesn't scare me. The last thing a tempter wants is his attention.

On to more pressing business, I see that your shadowing of the mother has borne some fruit. You stated that you observed a member of the heavenly host covertly aiding the woman. That tells us that she has enlisted the aid of the Creator.

She is still not saved. Her angelic helper wouldn't have been so subtle if she were. She still belongs to us indirectly. I did not appreciate where your report mentions that he seemed to look through a wall directly at you. I assure you, he was looking at you. He was telling you he was aware of you.

I found it even more disturbing that he played a game of cat and mouse with you for the rest of the day. You indicated that you didn't want him following you to your charge. That is a worthy goal but a futile one. If he is watching over the mother, he is already aware of her family's circumstances.

I suspect you were being herded. I don't think you realize this, but he appeared every time you said you started to go to the counselor's office. If I were to bet on this, I would say that he was trying to keep you from the counselor. That is disturbing, to say the least. This angel isn't only involved in the mother's affairs. He is also connected to the counselor somehow.

Remember what I told you about angels when you first came to me? I told you they spend so much time among the humans that they tend to take on their limitations. We are extra-dimensional creatures. They are as well. Humans can't fly, so they don't bother looking up a lot. They also don't look down a lot because the ground is solid to them.

Try using this the next time you want to check on the counselor. Long before you leave the gang, dive down into the earth. Give yourself a moment to get your bearings and simply flow through the ground to your destination. That is a trick we use to hide our activities from them.

It doesn't work every time, but sometimes it does. When it's all you have, you tend to use it.

Because of this situation, you were unable to get me information on the counseling session. I expect this to change. You will do what you can to lose your angelic shadow. If you are unsuccessful, you will proceed as though he isn't there. I want that information. What you've uncovered so far is only one piece in the puzzle.

So, we know that the heavenly host is butting into our business. I am hopeful that we are dealing with a single low-level angel. Angels are like wolves. You rarely see just one. They are usually in a pack, and they are always trouble for us.

In this instance, we can realistically hope that this single angel is another person's answer to prayer. Sometimes the Creator will dispatch an angel to watch over a human in a particular instance. It could be for protection. It could be to allow them to make a choice. He does take this free will thing seriously.

That was if we look at it optimistically. Now let's look at it realistically. It could very well be that our well-laid plans have been found out. This could be the tip of the iceberg. I don't like to say this at all. We must plan and act like everything is falling apart. If we don't, we stand a good chance of being caught off guard. I don't think I need to tell you that his lordship would be unhappy with us.

I will dispatch another five imps to you. You will use them with the rest of your imps. Put at least three on Carlos, three on Maria, and three on the mother. The rest will run messages back and forth to you. You will keep me apprised of this situation. Stay on your absolute top alert. We must assume we are working in hostile territory.

At this point, we desperately need information. If we are attacked by the heavenly host, there may be plans to move against his lordship. I will pass this information up the chain of command. You don't want to know what would happen to us if an attack came and we didn't report this information.

Deploy your imps. Keep in close contact. Report even the smallest details to me. We can't afford negligence at this point.

Your Infernal Mentor,

Shacklebolt

Master Tempter, I.T.B.

My Persistent tempter, Pinegrub,

During this turmoil, you managed to send me some good news. It is too bad you weren't there personally. It is always more satisfying when you are there during the event. Since Maria wasn't your charge, you could hardly have expected to be there. We can say, however, that this news sews up this loose end nicely!

I can't say I was surprised when I read that she had hanged herself. I was a bit surprised when you revealed she went to Carlos and threw his money back into his face before doing it. That reminds me a bit of Judas. Running away from the worst sin he ever committed and then committing suicide, attempting to atone or hide from it.

Your message explained how her mother found her, along with the note explaining why she'd done it. She mentioned that baby and Carlos. We can safely say that young man's troubles are far from over. From what you know, do you think it likely she will try to bring legal trouble to bear against him?

Your letter made no real mention of how Carlos is taking this news? Does he know? Does he have all the details? What was his reaction when she threw the money back into his face? He has been your charge for a while now. Can you tell if he is feeling guilty?

This event is something we can use against him for some time. If we play this correctly, we can crush his spirit with guilt for years. Whisper to him that he should have been more understanding. Tell him that her death and the baby's death are partly his fault. Keep an eye on him. When he seems to be handling things a bit better, bring these things back to the front of his memory.

You already stated that Maria's mother has her suicide note. What could you do to get that note into the hands of Carlos' mother? That would cause a delicious wave of despair. From what you've told me of the woman, this might be the thing that makes her give up on her son. Strange how words on a page can change a life.

It might be entertaining just to get that note to her. We could watch how she reacts. I'm sure it would cause her to be overly protective of her remaining children. It could easily cause her to hold on to her children so tightly that they pull away from her. Then would begin a downward spiral of the family tearing itself apart. The best part about that is we wouldn't have to do much to help it along.

I see the situation with the rival gang has come to a head. I consider it significant that Julian reacted so calmly. Four members of Los Jefes walking in to confront him is no small thing. Their hostile reaction to his interest in controlling a portion of their territory was no surprise. The leader being brave enough to walk into a Rival's headquarters with only three members to back him up is impressive.

I wonder what game Julian's tempter is playing. He could have motivated Julian to dispose of the rival gang members on the spot. The fact that he didn't tells me there are other plans. I need to speak with their Master Tempter in this case. I would not dispense with courtesy in this case. There may be well-laid plans that we are in danger of spoiling. Don't do anything to stir this up until I have investigated.

You observed that they walked in and confronted Julian with his intentions. He didn't deny their accusations. He did offer to negotiate for the territory. The offer of negotiation was rejected out of hand as expected. Julian must have known their rebuttal would be something like, "If you want our territory, take it if you can!"

You said that Julian believes they must strike soon. He doesn't want to give them time to fortify the area he wants. Does he know that Daniel is the one who leaked his plans? What is going on with the young traitor? I seem to remember he was in trouble with the leader of Los Jefes. Whatever came of that?

You said that soon means within the next week or so. Human terms like that bother me. They offer no exact information. That is akin to me telling you that I will reward you someday. A good leader provides concise information and instruction. We may have happened upon one of Julian's weak points. Was he indecisive when he made that statement?

You must attempt entangling Julian and Carlos even more now. Your charge is aware that Julian is Maria's cousin. He may be worried about the reaction of the gang leader to Maria's demise. Approach Julian's tempter and ask him to prompt Julian with Carlos' trustworthiness. Ask the tempter to give Julian the impression that he can rely upon your charge.

Your charge may be feeling overwhelmed. That is understandable with everything that has happened. Your concern at this point is to pile on more. Try to push Carlos more deeply into the gang. Have your imps prompt some of the other members to show confidence in him. That will give him a sense of belonging, which will cause him

189

to feel loyalty to the gang.

He has been away from his family environment. Use this situation to cause him to form false family bonds with those he thinks care. The closer we can pull him to these people, the more he will see his mother as unreasonable. He is only trying to take care of his family.

Concerning the mother, I am greatly disturbed that Mrs. Rodriguez has found employment with a Christian family. You successfully used the underground technique I described to you. That is good. What you discovered while using it is not. How did this happen? We had the entire family cut off! They were dependent on their strength to solve their problems.

My frustration stems from the fact that none of them had turned to the Creator. They weren't praying. They weren't asking for His help. Why suddenly did one of the heavenly hosts appear and take action? How did he do this so covertly? By your description, you almost tripped over him.

There must be someone in their lives that is saved. Whoever this person is, they are reaching out to the Father on their behalf. That is the only thing that makes sense. They don't even know they are lost.

The mother believes her prayers to the virgin Mary will be answered. Carlos believed that he was bending the rules for the greater good of his family. It wasn't until this business with Maria, her pregnancy, and the abortion until he realized he was lost. Afterward, he retreated into himself. He didn't suddenly start praying.

The only new element in their lives is the counselor that Carlos sees. He is the only element that we haven't been able to pin down. You were able to discover an angel, but you still haven't been able to attend a session of counseling. That sounds rather suspicious to me.

Here is what you are going to do. Task your imps to follow the angel. On the day that Carlos is to have counseling, you will stay with him all day. You will not leave his side under any circumstances. I think it is time we discover the nature of this counselor. Now get to work.

Your Infernal Mentor,

Shacklebolt

Master Tempter, I.T.B.

My gloriously victorious tempter, Pinegrub,

I must admit to a great deal of pleasure upon reading this last message. The way you influenced Julian to stab your charge to death was inspired. Your letter indicated that Julian asked your charge to be his second in the gang fight. When they faced off against the rival gang "Los Jefes," your charge would face their second, while Julian faced their leader.

You tempted Julian with the fact that if Carlos lost, he would have one less problem. Our research indicated that he was an opportunist. We didn't consider that he would be using a poisoned blade in a fight. Don't misunderstand me. His profile indicated a willingness to do anything to win. We just didn't consider him to be that imaginative. There's nothing like a little deceitful poison.

When he faced the leader of the rival gang, he did so with poison in his hand. That seems almost poetic. You must give him credit, he found the most toxic and fast-acting poison available. His blade was coated with, of all things, a potent insecticide. It just happened to be incredibly toxic to humans.

I especially liked your telling of the fight. Your description of Julian wholly giving himself to the fight was wonderful. At first, I thought you were overly embellishing, but you weren't. When he struck the killing strike against his opponent, you said he allowed you to see through his eyes. Proximity aided that since you were sitting on his shoulder.

You described a willing possession. I know, because of your past, you have no experience with this. You must have a human on the edge of insanity for them to consider that. That he eagerly allowed such a thing speaks volumes of your handling of him. I know the possession didn't last long, but it happened. I want you to realize, he can be your vessel in the future. Just keep that in mind.

You went on to describe how Carlos won his battle with the rival second. I liked how you describe his "plunge into darkness" as he took the life of his opponent. The look of remorse that you described on his face was priceless. Now that you have seen that look, you will recognize it every time you drag a human from their perceived grace.

At that moment, he felt that he'd crossed the uncrossable line. Almost all believing humans think they've committed the unforgivable sin. Even though they believe that the Savior died for their sins, they still believe this about themselves. It is hilarious.

I believe we both understand that it was pure luck that the betrayal happened right after Carlos felt he had betrayed his beliefs. Your description of the betrayal was excellent. Carlos and his opponent's fight had gone to the ground. They were thrashing wildly about until your charge was able to get behind his adversary. From there, it was a simple matter to choke the challenger to death.

The look of fear and reluctance becoming one of resignation and loss is almost priceless. In that single moment, you witnessed a human realizing he was betraying his most closely held beliefs. That was the look upon Judas Iscariot's face when he saw Christ being condemned to die.

In your account, you described how Carlos pushed his combatant's body off himself as he made to rise. It was then that Julian offered a helping hand that your charge accepted. Using encouraging words and a hand of fellowship, Julian stabbed your charge. Your description of how he twisted the poisoned blade was graphic.

I especially enjoyed your telling of how Julian spat upon Carlos before turning to walk away. I wasn't as surprised as you were that your charge cried out for his mother. Many of the so-called 'tough guys' do just that when death approaches.

I would have to say that the best part of your message by far was his prayer. Your charge knew that he was dying and didn't have the knowledge during his last moments to reach out to the Creator. He lay there clutching at his wound with the poison coursing through his body and prayed to the virgin Mary.

Your description of his waking to our existence was rather standard. Did you enjoy the moment that he became aware of you? Did you see the recognition on his face when he heard your voice? He realized that it was you talking to him all along. Wasn't his realization that he was among the damned precious to you?

You were able to reinforce false beliefs in one of the Creator's children. The ultimate blame for his choice to ignore the Holy Spirit's voice is his, but you affected his fate. That is something you will be able to carry with you for eternity.

Did you recognize any of the death angels that came to collect him? I have only recognized three in the long time that I've done this. It seems there are a great many soul collector angels. That only stands to reason since there are almost eight billion humans in this world. I assume you enjoyed his cries for mercy and prayers for help.

That is the one thing that you can't get across to the humans no matter how hard you try. Once the last breath is released, it is over. There are no more chances for forgiveness. Their test on this world is over, and there are no do-overs or extra credit. Yet, to a person, every unredeemed soul prays for forgiveness as they are being dragged away.

I must commend you on the timing of your charge's demise. Your description of the past two weeks justifies your action. I, personally, was unaware of the fact that Carlos's counselor was a Christian. It would seem he took great care to share the Gospel after spending time in prayer and supplication.

I am concerned about the lack of information on our part. Most Christians go about sharing the Gospel like a bulldozer going through the woods. It is all pomp and circumstance. They seem to scream, "Look at what I'm doing for the kingdom!" This instance wasn't like that. You are the first to bring us information on this counselor's activities.

Task several of your imps to watch this man. His position places him in ideal situations to share the good news of the Savior. That is not something we want to let go unchallenged. It is our business to make the recruiting of new Christians a hard job. I want more information on his habits and how he goes about broaching the subject of salvation.

In the meantime, I would like to inform you that you are being considered for a promotion. You have redeemed your worth, in my opinion. You have followed instructions well, and you have been creative in your own dealings. I am forwarding my recommendation up the chain of command to promote you to Tempter First Class.

I am recommending that your next charge be Andre, Carlos' younger brother. You are familiar with the family already. That should make it all the easier to drag him to damnation once he reaches the age of accountability. You are to keep your distance from the young man until then.

Until that time is upon us, I would like you to keep track of this counselor. Find out whatever you can about him. I also want you to keep the imps you currently have on Carlo's mother right where they are. If it is approved that your next charge is Andre, you will have less setup work to do. Since it is less work, we love to keep corruption and damnation in the family.

In the meantime, you need to prepare for your awards dinner. This was your first time demonstrating that you have what you need to corrupt a human soul. You will be honored for your first real achievement. Enjoy the accolades. They don't come often to our kind.

Your Infernal Mentor,

Shacklebolt

Master Tempter, I.T.B.

A word from the author

I realize this has been upsetting to some of the readers. This book was written to provide a realistic and Biblical premise of fallen human behavior and our reactions to invisible enemies working tirelessly against us. This book is meant to inform the reader of a reality that we can't perceive but that the Bible warns us.

A terrifying thought given to us from the Bible is that there are a great many who will not make it into Heaven.

Matthew 7:13 "Enter through the narrow gate. For wide is the gate and broad is the road that leads to destruction, and many enter through it. But small is the gate and narrow the road that leads to life, and only a few find it."

Jesus told his disciples, "I am the way, the truth, and the life. No one comes to the Father except through me." According to the Word of God, Jesus is the only way to God. Also, salvation is an unwarranted gift for those who are willing to receive it. Receiving it doesn't mean you accept it and go on about your business. It also doesn't mean you have to work hard to earn it.

Nothing that you can do will add to or take away from your salvation. You can't be good enough to earn it, and after you have it, you can't screw up enough to lose it. I know that some of you reading this will be Christians. I also suspect that some of you will wonder about some of the less than savory things you've done since you became a Christian. Consider this.

If you could lose your salvation, you would. We, as fallen humans, are naturally geared toward sin. You have to teach a child to tell the truth. You don't have to teach them to lie. Self-preservation will show them how to lie. When a child does something they believe they will get into trouble for, they almost automatically lie about it.

"Did you break that cup?" Dad asked. "No Daddy, I promise I didn't do it." How many times have you seen or heard something like that? That is only an example of what a child will do. Adults who know better lie almost casually.

Have you ever lied to keep from hurting someone's feelings? Have you ever lied to keep a fight from starting? Have you ever lied to keep yourself out of trouble? I can answer honestly that I've done all three. I do not make a habit of lying, but sometimes when you are in a situation, it is almost automatic. I am not condoning this behavior. I am just describing human nature.

It only took one act of disobedience to get Adam and Eve cast out of the Garden. How much more would we be cast out if all our sins were laid bare? Let's be nicer about it and say only the ones since we were saved. That would still be way more than enough to have us cast away from the Lord's presence.

The most terrifying thing to a person professing to be a Christian is this passage. Matthew 7:21-23 says: Not everyone who says to me, 'Lord, Lord,' will enter the kingdom of heaven, but only the one who does the will of my Father who is in heaven. Many will say to me on that day, "Lord, Lord, did we not prophesy in your name and in your name drive out demons, and in your name perform many miracles?" Then I will tell them plainly, "I never knew you. Away from me, you evildoers!"

This seems to be a warning to those who "get saved" and then live their lives according to their own moral code. They've given a nod to the Lord as God. They accept the gift of salvation probably mainly out of fear and think they are covered. The problem is that they haven't given their heart to the Lord. They may give to the poor, but it is out of a sense of obligation. They may visit the sick or feed their neighbor, but it is more out of a sense of obeying the law, not honoring their Lord that saved them.

The best thing about salvation is that it DOESN'T DEPEND ON US. God is the author and finisher of our salvation. It is by His mercy and His word that we are saved. Be thankful to the Lord that you can't affect your salvation. Be thankful that once you have the gift of salvation, it is yours.

If you have repented of your sins and acknowledged Jesus Christ as Lord and Savior, then rejoice because you are saved. If you haven't, then what is holding you back?

For those who are already saved, do you love your unsaved friends? The last command Jesus gave before he ascended was to make disciples of all nations. It is unpopular, can be awkward, and, depending on the person, sometimes unpleasant. Here is a final thought. If someone you barely knew stood in the middle of a busy street, unaware of the traffic about to hit them, would you at least warn them?